DEADLY DANGER

Mystery and Suspense on Santa Rosa Island

MARK C. PILLES

Mayhaven Publishing, Inc.
P. O. Box 557
Mahomet, IL 61853
USA

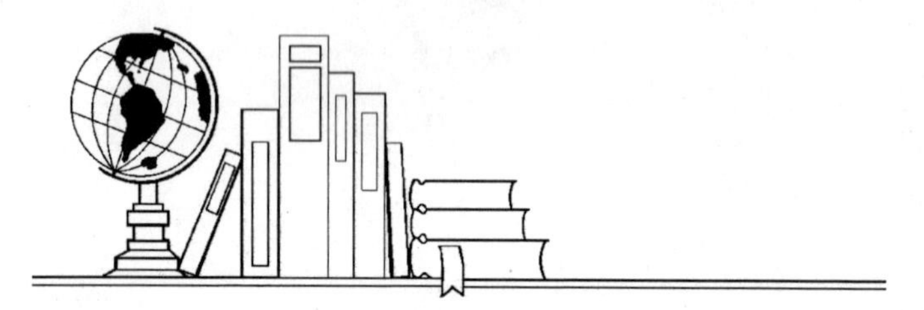

Cover and Text Page Photographs: Harry G. Wenzel
Cover Design: Doris Replogle Wenzel

Library of Congress Control Number: 2013939483
First Edition—First Printing 2013
ISBN 13 978 193227842-2

Mark C. Pilles

For Sandy

Mark C. Pilles

TABLE OF CONTENTS

Mark C. Pilles

PROLOGUE

Sierra Madre Mountains, Mexico — August 24, 1886

There were not many of them left, about fifty Apaches from various bands including White Mountain, Chiricahuas and Nednais — hiding in the lava fields and ravines of northern Mexico. Those the Mexican Army did not kill died from natural causes. The rest made their way back to the reservation at San Carlos, Arizona.

And now, through an agreement with the Mexican government, the United States Army was closing in on them, making it harder and harder for the warriors to slip past the endless sea of blue shirts to find food and clothing.

That afternoon a teenage Apache on guard spotted two Indian scouts serving with the U.S. Army riding towards them. A white flour sack tied to a pole fluttered high in the air.

"Kill them!" Apache leader Geronimo ordered.

"No! They are of our blood. Let us hear their words," a brave responded.

Geronimo nodded.

He heard what he already knew. "You have no place to go. You have no friends. If you keep running, we will kill the very last one of you — even if it takes fifty years. Lay down your arms, surrender, live in peace."

The Apache leader looked beyond his exhausted group to the

blood red mountains on the horizon. There was no talk among the Indians. They knew what must be done. Geronimo sent a reply. He wished to parley with Lieutenant Charles B. Gatewood who represented General Nelson A. Miles.

The conference was held at the Army's camp on the Bivispe River. And on September 3, 1886, the most feared Indian warrior of all time surrendered to General Miles. The Apache War was over.

Ft. Pickens — Santa Rosa Island, Florida — May 1, 1888

"Where are you taking us?" Geronimo asked his guard Private Jacob S. McCoy.

"We're transfering you to Mount Vernon barracks in Alabama," Private McCoy answered quickly.

"When will we go?"

The soldier looked at Geronimo, his wives and the rest of the Apaches with sympathetic eyes.

"Soon," McCoy replied.

"We will be ready when you say."

As the soldier was leaving he saw Geronimo take a small faded pouch, tied with a leather thong, from his pocket and walk over to the salt encrusted southern wall of Ft. Pickens. A half hour later, when the soldier returned, he noticed a small amount of red mortar dust on the floor. Geronimo was wiping his hands.

Private Jacob McCoy claimed he knew what was in that pouch and vowed to return to Ft. Pickens and retrieve it. The soldier never did make it back to Florida. Instead, he lived to be a very old man, after swearing his family to secrecy about the location of "Geronimo's gold."

MEET THE DEVIL

Ft. Pickens — Santa Rosa Island, Florida — The Present

"He knows the secret." Warren Chapman licked a blackened marshmallow from a stick, shoved another on it, and stuck the stick back into the fire. Orange flames from the campfire reflected off his dark skin and the whites of his eyes.

"Like who, Mr. Chapman?" Fourteen-year-old Wendy Terrell asked. "And what secret?"

"That old fisherman, Bucky McCoy." Chapman leaned closer to Wendy. "He's the only person alive who knows where Geronimo stashed his gold."

"So what?" Wendy took a sip of Pepsi. "I don't know any Bucky McCoy or anything about any gold." Wendy put a hot dog on a stick and stuck it in the middle of a flickering flame. Her tongue, nose and lip rings gleamed in the firelight. The light vaguely revealed her mild acne.

"Geronimo was a prisoner at Ft. Pickens. That's where he hid his gold." Twenty-two-year-old Chapman pulled his stick from the fire, pulled the flaming marshmallow off with his teeth, then threw the stick into the burning logs. He pulled a pack of Winstons from his shirt pocket, tapped out a cigarette and lit it. "I know the gold's there but I need to know the exact location."

"Like what does that have to do with me?" Wendy laid her hotdog in a bun then pulled out the stick.

Chapman inhaled. "You're smart, pretty, and sometimes friendly. Hang around his fishing boat, become his friend, earn his trust, and get him to tell you where the gold is."

"How will I know him?"

"Bucky carries a pelican around with him and has only one or two teeth."

Chapman's wife Sally plucked the cigarette from her husband's hand, then continued carrying a bowl of potato salad to a nearby table.

Wendy wrinkled up her nose. "Like, what's in it for me?"

Chapman lit another cigarette. "Part of the gold, of course."

Wendy's eyes brightened. "Alright!"

"Puh-lease. Don't make me laugh." In the glow of the firelight, thirteen-year-old Rusty Parker rolled his eyes. That's all I need, he thought. Besides, that Geronimo's gold thing is a myth. Cal Sapp said so, and his dad is boss here at Ft. Pickens. Rusty licked the last bit of gooey confection off his stick and looked up at the full moon.

"Stephen Walter Parker! You ate almost all of the marshmallows!" Rusty's mother Diane, held up an empty plastic bag.

"Sorry."

"That's why you're so fat," Wendy quipped.

"Bite me."

"Rusty! Don't talk to your cousin like that," Diane threw the bag into the fire and picked up a spatula.

"Tell her not to talk to me that way."

"You heard me." Diane, spatula in one hand and the other hand on her hip, glared at Rusty.

"I can start tomorrow, Mr. Chapman." Wendy held out her hand. "Deal?"

Chapman blew a smoke ring then gave Wendy a limp handshake. "Deal. And call me Warren since we're business partners."

It was too much. Rusty got up, cast a glance at the bright stars and full moon, said goodnight to his mother, who was laughing with Sally, then headed for their RV. "I'm going inside."

How gullible can you get? Rusty turned the faucet on, squeezed the toothpaste onto his brush and began brushing his teeth. When it came to money Wendy would do anything. She had money but she couldn't touch it until she was eighteen. It was true, he decided, people with money want more money. Now Wendy was falling for this story and, because some guy asked her to be his partner, she more than willingly agreed. Serves her right! Rusty rinsed his mouth and smiled self-righteously at the mirror.

Before putting on his pajamas, Rusty looked at the mirror one more time, and ran his fingers through his cinnamon hair. His round body, and chubby, freckled face, stared back at him. Mom and the doctor say I have to lose weight. They don't get it. I'm trying. Instead of two peanut butter and jelly sandwiches, I'm down to one and a half and I'm eating only six Oreos instead of twelve.

Tired of helping his mother set up camp, tired of doing both his and Wendy's chores, which included gathering firewood, Rusty was asleep before his head hit the pillow. He was having a pretty nice dream when he felt a hand on his shoulder — shaking him.

"Hey fatso, you awake?" Wendy asked.

"No, I'm havin' a nightmare about you. Bug off."

"You big tub of lard. Are you going to help me?"

"Help you do what?" Rusty yawned.

"Find the gold, stupid."

"No. Now be quiet. You'll wake up Mom."

"You'll be sorry, fat boy, when I find that gold. I'll be rich," Wendy taunted.

"You're the one who'll be sorry if you get caught, 'cause diggin' on federal property is against the law."

"Who said?"

"Cal said."

Wendy shrugged. "Your loss."

Rusty lay awake a long time after that. Why did Mom agree to bring her along? It was supposed to be a family vacation: Dad, Mom and me — not evil incarnate Wendy Terrell — Now, she's going to New Orleans for Dad's newscaster job interview. Oh sure, she's family — a cousin or something like that. Not a sister, thank god!

Why did the RV have to break down? Why is it taking so long to get the part? And why do I have to listen to Wendy's insults? All the way up from Lakeland, when Mom and Dad were out of hearing range, she ragged on me. Then, when they're around she's usually as sweet as pie. Sort of like Eddie Haskell on that ancient TV show, *Leave it to Beaver*. When the "Beav" was with the boys Eddie tormented him unmercifully, but when Eddie was around Beaver's parents he was as nice as could be. The only thing is, Eddie Haskell was fake. Wendy is real.

Rusty sighed, got up and looked out the window of the motor home at the campsite next door. The Chapmans huddled close to the campfire and had what looked like a map on their laps. It had to be after midnight. Rusty pushed the stem on his watch, and the face lit a dark blue. Closer to 3 a.m. Shouldn't they be asleep?

Oh well. Rusty crawled back in bed, pulled his pillow close to him and closed his eyes. If Wendy is happy chasing that stupid story more power to her — as long as it doesn't involve me. Suddenly he opened his eyes and frowned. Why do I get the feeling I'm going to be involved whether I like it or not?

NOT BAD FOR A GEEK

Ft. Pickens - Santa Rosa Island, Florida

As Rusty finished dishes for the third time in a row, (Wendy would get her hands wrinkled), he saw her wipe off her bicycle seat.

Diane watched her niece hang the rag on a tree limb, then poured herself a cup of coffee. “Rusty, I wish you would go with your cousin. She mentioned something about talking to a fishing guide.”

“Why? Cal and I were goin’ to take his boat out. I’d like to catch a snook. I’ve never been in the Gulf before, remember?” Rusty wiped his hands on a towel then hung it on the cabinet door.

“I remember but I don’t like her going anywhere in this strange place alone.” The look his mother gave him settled the question.

“Oh, alright, but you owe me.”

When Rusty went out to take his bike down off the rack. He looked west towards New Orleans. Thanks Dad, thanks for leaving me with this demon seed — and thanks for making this the total vacation from hell.

Rusty caught up with Wendy a little way from the campsite.

Wendy shot him a dirty look. “Do you have to follow me?”

“Believe me, I didn’t want to. Mom made me,” Rusty said.

“What a good little boy,” Wendy sneered. “ ‘Mom made me.’ I’ll have to have a talk with that woman.” Wendy pushed down on the pedal, her black and purple hair blowing in the breeze.

Rusty took off after her, his heart pounding. He gasped for breath as he tried to keep up. Sweat dropped down his forehead and stung as it pooled in his eyes. Every time Wendy saw him gaining on her she sped up. The fiery mid-morning sun beat down on both of them, cooking the asphalt and burning their arms, legs and faces while sucking every drop of moisture from their bodies. Heat distorted the asphalt causing a wavy wet appearance. Finally, at the Pensacola Beach city-limit sign, the heat got to Wendy and she stopped.

"I'm hot." She nodded to an ice cream parlor with tables and umbrellas. The tables sat on a patio that bordered the Gulf. "Let's get something to drink."

They sat at a table with the Gulf behind them. A large sign with a picture of a double milkshake, topped with whipped cream, filled the left side of the menu and pictures of bacon cheeseburgers and chili-dogs took up the right side.

Gosh, Rusty stared at the picture, his mouth drooling. I wish I could have that double chocolate milkshake with all that whipped cream and a double bacon cheeseburger — but instead I'll have a Diet Coke and that's it. At least I'll be proud of myself.

Wendy ordered the double milkshake. "Ummmm," she grinned as it was placed in front of her. Rusty turned away as she tauntingly put the cherry between her teeth and plucked out the stem.

Rusty closed his eyes and listened to the sounds of the beach: jet skis, seagulls and people laughing and shouting. He was almost asleep when he heard a crackling voice say, "Yeah, I know where Gerony-mo's gold is. Why, my great granddaddy was Gerony-mo's personal guard."

Rusty and Wendy turned toward their right and saw a weathered old man in a chair holding a plastic cup, containing a light brown something, on the floor by his left foot. A pelican with a white head, and a yellow spot on the back of its neck, dozed restlessly nearby. Occasionally the bird yawned as if bored, haveing heard the story a thousand times before. Once in a while it flapped its wings then returned to its nap.

The man didn't seem to notice the bird. His skin looked like leather, his face, arms and hands were covered with spots from a lifetime of being in the sun and on the water. Only two upper, and three lower, yellowed teeth showed.

Rusty sized him up. The old guy isn't smoking. Probably chews. And as there's no foam on the brown liquid in the cup, it's definitely not soda.

About a dozen people nursed their refreshments and listened to the old man.

"Then why haven't you got the gold, Bucky?" a man asked.

"Cain't. Not with all them govy-ment people around."

"Why aren't you working?" Another voice asked.

"Why, a man's gotta have a little time to himself, don't ye think?" the old man shot back.

"I think you tell a pretty good story when you're drunk." The group broke into laughter.

"C'mon, Norma Jean." Bucky McCoy grabbed his cup and the bird and got up. "I know when we're not wanted." The pelican nestled on Bucky's shoulder as he shuffled off.

Wendy watched the old fisherman leave and slurped the rest of her milkshake. "See ya," she said, leaving Rusty to pay the bill.

Great. Rusty finished his soda and fished in his pants pocket for some money. He paid the bill, leaving the few cents change as a tip. The waitress gave him a dirty look as he followed Wendy. Just great, he thought. Just great.

Wendy left her bike where it was and walked a few feet behind the old fishing guide who was mumbling to himself and the pelican. Rusty followed her on foot. When she heard Rusty huffing and puffing to catch up, she turned and frowned, motioning him to be quiet.

Soon the marinas came into view. On the north, the Escambia Bay side, yachts like *Ramblin' Rose* bobbed gently at their moorings. Painted white, blue and all colors in between, their masts reached toward the sun. On the south, the Gulf side, the fishing boats were docked. People were boarding and unboarding the vessels. Some stood under a rack smiling as their picture was taken with their catch: a large grouper, a bunch of trout and a shark or two.

Down about two slips, a wooden sign with cracked white paint hung over a pier. Faded black letters spelled out: CAPT. BUCKY McCOY'S FISHING CHARTER. WHOLE AND HALF DAY RATES.

"Hey Chubby, you can go now. See ya." Wendy waited until Bucky McCoy and Norma Jean were on deck before she approached. In contrast to the sign, the boat's brass glimmered in the sunlight. The name *SilverKing* was trimmed in fresh black paint on both sides of the bow. Hardly a rust spot showed on the brilliant white hull.

A feeling that something wasn't right crept over Rusty. He looked towards the Gulf then back towards the campsite and didn't see anything abnormal. He looked towards the mainland and everything seemed okay, there. He looked at the parking lot and that's where he saw them. A thin man in a polo shirt, slacks, and wearing aviator sunglasses, leaned against the hood of a red Dodge Charger with his arms folded. He looked like he was asleep. A second man, with the look of a body builder, worked a wad of gum as he watched a man Rusty judged to be in his mid-twenties, wearing a tattered Beatles' "Let it Be" T-shirt and ragged jeans, follow the old fishing guide around.

"Wait, Wendy," Rusty whispered. "Something's up."

"Right, fat boy," Wendy laughed sarcastically. "Don't try that crap with me."

Norma Jean waddled alongside the old fisherman's feet. Another, even younger man, wearing a pair of cut-off jean shorts and a black Red Sox baseball cap worked a line in the bow and frequently looked at the two men on deck. His coal-black hair protruding from his cap shined in the noonday sun while sweat glistened on his tanned muscular back and arms. When he saw Wendy he smiled, showing a mouthful of ivory teeth. Wendy seemed to ignore him although Rusty did see her quick smile.

"Listen." Rusty nodded to the two men — now arguing. Wendy heard them, too, and paused halfway up the gangway.

"I'd like to help ye, Noah, but I cain't." The old fishing guide lifted the lid to the live bait well, looked inside, then closed it.

"Please, Bucky, I need to be on this boat. I'll take half pay. I just want to be with you until that outdoor reporter job comes through with the newspaper." He followed McCoy around the deck — careful not to step on Norma Jean.

"What happened to thet govy-ment job ye had?" The fishing guide picked up a rod and reel and inspected it.

"Budget cuts and all. Please, Bucky. Tricia is killing me. She's always taking me to court. Wants money for this, money for that. The kids need new soccer gear, braces, all kinds of stuff. I don't have an extra dime to my name."

"Heh-heh. Me and Pap told ye not to marry thet girl. Told ye she was nuthin' but trouble."

The young man threw his hands up. "Alright, alright. You and Pappy were right. I was wrong, but I deserve a second chance. Put me on, Bucky."

"I cain't. Look, I'm gonna be honest with ye. The bank is fixin' to foreclose on this here boat. If it weren't for me givin' Tommy Plummer some grouper every time I can I'd be on land now. If you're all fired up to come back fishin' and guidin', try Ben Casswell. He'll put ye on."

"Okay. I can see I'm not gettin' through." Noah ran his arm across his forehead. "Alright. Just do me one favor, stop your drinking. That's affecting your business."

"Never has, never will."

"Oh for . . ." Noah stormed off the boat and past Wendy and Rusty without noticing them.

"What happened?" The big man with muscles asked.

"Forget about it." Noah got in the back seat and slammed the door. The Charger scratched gravel as it sped off.

"Rory, how's our liquid ree-freshments?" Bucky asked the much younger deck hand.

"Beer, soda and ice filled to the brim, Cap'n." Rory didn't even look up from the bow.

"Very good." McCoy weaved slightly.

The movement caught Rory's attention. "Are you okay, Cap'n?"

"I'm fine, I'm fine. Just tend to ye work."

The two cousins looked at each other then Rusty walked toward the *SilverKing* gangplank. Bucky McCoy was hosing down the deck, Norma Jean still waddling alongside him. When he looked up, he saw Wendy and Rusty.

"C'mon aboard," he waved. "Thet fella that jist left was my kid brother. Lazy as the day is long. Not like Rory, there."

Again, Rory made eyes at Wendy. This time Wendy smiled openly.

Here we go again, Rusty thought.

The captian held out his hand. "I'm Bucky McCoy. Who might you be?"

The cousins introduced themselves. Norma Jean squawked.

"I'm sorry, Norma Jean. Kids, this here's Norma Jean. Smartest pelican this side of the Mississippi. Found her tangled up in fishin' line 'bout half dead. She's all the family I have in this world and thet includes my kid brother."

Rory cleared his throat.

"Oh, and thet's Rory, my first mate."

Rory walked over and shook Rusty's hand, then took Wendy's hand, and lightly kissed it. "Charmed," he said softly.

Wendy tittered and attempted to blush.

~~Damnit!~~ Rusty looked at Wendy in disgust. The way she's acting you'd think she never saw a guy before.

Rory asked McCoy if he could go ashore and purchase some supplies for the boat. The old fishing guide gave his permission. The first mate gave Wendy a mocking salute then leapt to the dock.

Wendy dreamily watched Rory fade into the distance then looked at the pelican. "Smartest pelican east of the Mississippi?" She rolled her eyes. "O-okay."

"Ye don't believe me?" The old fishing guide smiled. "Watch this. Norma Jean, how much is two times four."

Norma Jean tapped the highly polished deck eight times with her beak.

"Good." McCoy gave her a fish. "Now watch. How much is five take away two?"

The pelican tapped three.

"Well, I'll be." Rusty shook his head.

"Ye new'round here?" McCoy went back to hosing the deck.

"Well . . ." Rusty made a face. "Sort of." Rusty told the fishing guide their story.

Norma Jean waddled closer and Wendy backed up.

"She likes ye and wants ye to feed her," Bucky said.

"I don't have anything to give her." The pelican gained on Wendy. She backed up further, until she was against the gunwale.

"Do ye want to feed her?"

"I . . . I . . ." Wendy looked at the pelican's beak then her eyes. "I guess.

"One pinfish." Bucky reached into the live well and handed Wendy a small silver and yellow fish.

"E-eww!" Wendy backed away.

"Take it!" The old fishing guide ordered. The fish flopped violently in McCoy's hand. Wendy grabbed it by the tail with two fingers, and in one swift motion flung the fish at the bird. Norma Jean gobbled it down, her large pouch jiggling as she swallowed. Then she waddled up to Wendy for more.

"That's enough, Norma Jean," the old fishing guide said. "You'll spoil yer dinner."

The pelican waddled back to McCoy.

It didn't take Wendy long to get to the point. "Mr. err . . . Captain McCoy, since we're, like, stranded here for awhile can I . . ." She looked at Rusty. ". . . or we . . . help you on your boat? I could babysit Norma Jean. It could be like, for nothing."

"Norma Jean don't need no babysitter." McCoy shut the faucet off and began coiling the hose. "But it might not be a bad idee — free help. Rory could use a hand and ye could learn something, too. Young lady, be here at six — tomorrow morning. Nice to have met ye." He wiped his hands and went below.

Rusty thought Wendy's chin would touch the ground just as Rory came back with a paper bag full of potato chips, beef jerky and a jar of pickled eggs.

"Six tomorrow morning?" Wendy mouthed. "Rory's back so I'm gonna hang out here for awhile."

"What do I tell Mom?" Rusty watched Rory go inside with the bag then shook his head. What sane person would eat pickled eggs while out on the water?

"Think of something, stupid." Wendy scoffed at Rusty's remark and followed Rory into the cabin.

Rusty laughed to himself all the way back to the RV as he remembered the look on Wendy's face.

Back at the campsite, after Wendy returned, Diane suggested they search for more firewood.

"Bor-ing," Wendy sighed and mozied after her cousin.

Rusty walked down the white quartz road, seeing and hearing the waves of the Gulf of Mexico ebb and flow on his left. He took a deep breath of salt air. It smelled and felt good. To his right, a short line of pine, palm, oak, and various shrubs and bushes, lined the road. Before long Rusty had an armful of scrub oak. Wendy had nothing. Struggling back to camp with his burden he found one more short log under a tree.

"Grab it, Wendy," he puffed, noticing the Chapman's Nissan was gone.

"I might break a nail."

"For gosh sakes!" Anger roiled up in Rusty's stomach. His face turned red. "You won't break a nail, Wendy."

"I will."

At camp Rusty dropped the load of wood under a tree with the rest of the firewood, not caring whether it was stacked or not, then walked towards the beach. Rusty's mother watched him then looked at Wendy sashaying up in her baggy black pants.

"Wendy, you could have helped Rusty," Diane said.

"I'd get dirty."

"I know, but you have to pull your weight on this trip."

Wendy kicked the ground. "I didn't even want to come on this dumb trip anyway."

"But you're here. Try to make the best of a bad situation."

"It sucks!" She hurried into the motor home.

It was always the same, Rusty thought. Mom'll cave in. She always does. It's been that way forever. Even on the trip up from Lakeland. Dad and I wanted to stop at a barbecue place but no, Wendy had to stop at *Wendy's* and Mom agreed. Then there was that cool computer store Dad and I wanted to stop at for a minute but no, Wendy wanted to stop at a mall and Mom caved in. To think Aunt Susan said Wendy would be no problem. Wendy came along just so Aunt Susan could spend some time with her new boyfriend — to 'get to know him better,' she'd said.

No problem? Getting a D and an F on your report card, and being grounded for a month, was not a problem — compared to Wendy.

Breaking your leg and having it in a cast for six months was not a problem — compared to Wendy. In fact, no disaster on earth was a problem — compared to Wendy.

Rusty ignored the motor scooters and hikers passing him until he heard the unmistakable sound of bicycle tires crunching on shells behind him.

"What's up?" Cal Sapp stopped beside Rusty. His olive skin and black hair glistened in the sun. Rusty remembered Cal telling him that he was a three-quarter Cherokee.

"My stupid cousin, that's what."

"Huh?"

"She doesn't help out at the RV, she thinks she's God's gift to boys, yet she always gets her way. My aunt and uncle are divorced and she pits them against each other and wins. Now she's pitting my parents against each other and my mom against me!"

"Have you tried talkin' to your mom about this when she's in a good mood?"

"She won't listen. To her Wendy can do no wrong."

"You never know. Women are funny." Cal got off his bike and stretched.

"I'm findin' that out."

"I had a cousin like that," Cal said.

"What happened to her?"

"Him. I dunno. We moved." Cal thought for a moment then said, "Wendy is sorta cute."

"Who?"

"Wendy." Cal got back on his bike and blew a lock of hair off his forehead.

Rusty shrugged. To each his own. "Now, get this. Some fool at the campground put her on to finding Geronimo's gold and she's all hip to find out where it is from this fishing guide called Bucky McCoy. And this old guy's first mate is making eyes at Wendy and she's goin' ga-ga over that."

Cal stopped short. "Bucky McCoy's first mate? Rory Abrams?"

Rusty began pedaling. "Don't know his last name, but yeah, Rory's his first name."

"Wendy needs to be careful, Rusty. Rory ain't the nicest guy in the world." Cal looked towards Ft. Pickens. "Does she know there is no gold?"

"Nah, she's so taken in with that Chapman dude she wouldn't listen to us anyway." Rusty wiped the sweat from his forehead. His stomach grumbled. "What d'ya wanna do after we eat?"

"Eat? I just had lunch. We can't take my skiff out 'cause my dad is usin' it. The Fourth is in a couple of days. Wanna get some fireworks?"

"Okay." Rusty looked at the Gulf. Raven-colored clouds hung low over the water. Lightening lanced the Gulf and thunder grumbled in the distance. "Let me get my poncho and some money."

Back at the RV, Wendy decided to tag along. "I'll race you, Cal." She smiled.

"You're gonna lose." Cal scratched off, getting a head start on Wendy and leaving Rusty sitting on his bike watching. Wendy tossed her head back, her laughter ringing in the breeze at something Cal said. Rusty took off, pedaling as fast as possible. He could hear Wendy shouting at Cal and Cal yelling back. Rusty saw the admiring look Wendy gave Cal, and sadly looked at his pedals and the road. No girl will ever look at me like that, he thought.

At the fireworks tent Rusty bought some bottle rockets, cherry bombs, and some spirals. Cal bought the same while Wendy looked up and down the aisles. Rusty walked over to the more elaborate fireworks and saw Wendy pick up a package, say something to Cal, giving him a wondering look, then put the package down. She wound up buying a few sparklers.

Rusty put the fireworks deep in the pockets of his poncho then went back to his bike.

"Do y'all wanna ride to Pensacola Beach?" Cal asked.

"Oh yeah, I think we passed a tattoo parlor on the way in. I want a tattoo," Wendy said.

Rusty got on his bike. "I don't think you're old enough for one, Wendy."

"Rory has one of a dragon on his leg so I want one of a sorceress. And do you have to join us, Rusty?"

"Why not? It's my vacation, too," Rusty answered. "And for you, a Daffy Duck tattoo would be more like it."

Cal bit back a laugh.

"It's just you're . . . you're so retarded."

"He is not, Wendy. He's more than welcome to join us," Cal added.

"He's going to spy on us and tell Aunt Diane."

"Why? There's nothin' to spy about," Cal said.

"Why would I spy on a dork?" Rusty shot back.

"Maybe we should go home," Cal suggested.

"No. Let's go. I won't tell Mom," Rusty said.

"Promise?" Wendy asked.

"Promise." Rusty nodded.

"Hey," Wendy had to get the last jab, "you're not bad for a geek."

The remark stung Rusty like a slap in the face. It's bad enough to call me names, but to do it in front of a new friend is ignorant, Rusty thought. So what if I like computer and video games, and like to read mysteries and watch detective shows better than hanging out at the mall? So what if I'm a little, well, more than a little overweight and can't dance? What few friends I have are good friends, tried and true, not the store-bought kind Wendy hangs around with. No, one day I'll prove I'm alright. One day I'll prove I'm cool. One day, one day . . .

A GUT FEELING

Santa Rosa Island, Florida

Rusty waded into the warm water of the Gulf and cast out. It feels good to be alone, he thought. Peace and quiet. The only sounds were the waves lapping, mullet leaping out of the water, and seagulls screeching. In the distance, a pod of dolphins launched themselves out of the water then dropped back in and swam happily on to their next adventure. He flicked his pole and watched the line, with a piece of frozen shrimp he bought at WalMart attached to the hook, sail through the air then plop into the water. Rusty smiled, satisfied he'd made a good cast and admired the vanishing dolphins. The smile faded as he pondered the remarks Wendy had made. His thoughts wandered.

As far back as I can remember Wendy has picked on me. Why, I don't know. I've always treated her decently but the kind treatment has almost always been returned with insults she throws back at me — and they're downright nasty. No one's said anything to her about it either. Only Dad has ever made an attempt to stand up to her — once — and that was pretty weak. And when Mom took Wendy's side, Mom and Dad started fighting. I can hear the argument, now: "For God's sake Diane, he's our son. He can't be wrong all the time. Have some backbone and stick up for him once in awhile."

"Oh, I know. But Wendy has had such a rough time of it," Mom answered back.

Then Dad said, “And she’s taking advantage of every single minute of it.”

Finally, either Mom or Dad slammed the door and that was it. I think for the sake of peace, Dad had given up.

Rusty felt a tug on his hook and saw the pole bend. He set the hook with a quick jerk but whatever it was broke free. He reeled in only to find his bait gone.

“Use a smaller hook and one of these.”

Rusty almost bolted out of the water, nearly dropping his fishing pole in fright. He turned and saw Noah McCoy standing behind him holding a tiny bait fish. “Try this.”

“Thanks. Be right back.” Rusty waded ashore and over to his tackle box while Noah watched a catamaran in the distance. Rusty changed hooks, ran the point through the bait fish’s nose, then went back into the water and cast out.

“I saw you at my brother’s boat yesterday.” Noah’s eyes fastened on Rusty. “What were you and that girl doing there?”

Rusty turned to look at him. What’s going on? Rusty thought. An uneasy feeling crept over him. “Nothing much.”

“Sorry.” Noah shrugged and grinned. “So, why were you there?”

“Your brother gave my cousin a job — sorta. But she’s workin’ for nothin.” Suddenly, Rusty’s pole bent and started shaking.

“For nothing, aye?” Noah ignored the boy’s fight. “Why would she do a thing like that?”

The fish gave no quarter — fighting as hard as it could. Rusty shouted back over his shoulder, “She believes your brother knows where Geronimo’s gold is hidden.”

“That . . .” Noah shook his head and snorted. “has been a family plague for the last century. Who told her about the gold?"

Rusty found it harder and harder to reel in. The line veered to the left for a few seconds then ran to the right. Every time Rusty gained an inch the fish took two inches. "I dunno."

"Oh? She just came home and said, 'I'm going to dig for Geronimo's gold?' " Noah watched Rusty fight the fish. "Give 'em some slack. So, someone told her. Could it be someone at the campground?"

Rusty stood stock still. "How do you know where we're stayin'?"

"It's a small island and pretty close to my home. Look, I can dig it, if you don't want to tell me, but listen to me." Noah McCoy put his hand on Rusty's shoulder. "I don't know how long you're going to be in Pensacola, but it's in your best interest for you and your cousin to keep away from my brother. That — and your cousin needs to keep away from Rory Abrams, too."

"Why?" Rusty finally pulled in a sixteen-inch gafftop catfish.

"Nice cat. Here." Noah pulled a handkerchief from his pocket. "Put it over the dorsal fin so you don't get cut and ease back on it. In answer to your question, just take my word for it, okay?"

Rusty nodded then put the handkerchief on the front of the razor-sharp fin, pushed down and back. He removed the hook and set the fish free.

"I have to go. Keep the hanky," Noah said, turning toward the dunes.

"Thanks." Rusty watched him walk away then, as an afterthought, hollered, "Hey, where can I catch a snook?"

Noah stopped and turned. "Any place. But you better not."

"Why?"

"Season's closed."

Deadly Danger

Rusty looked at his empty hook, and at Noah McCoy growing smaller in the distance. Hmmm, if a catfish eats a bait fish or a shiner, surely a snook would scarf 'em down. I'll have to go to a bait shop at the marina and buy some. Anyway, my fishin' is over for the day.

Rusty waded to shore, picked up his tackle box and headed back to the campsite. He thought about Noah's warning. Why should we stay away from Bucky McCoy? Was he after something? That look on his face, when I told him Wendy was working for nothing, said a lot. We heard him say he didn't have an extra dime to his name. Did he really need a job that bad? And that thing about Geronimo's gold being a family plague — somethin's not right.

Approaching the RV, Rusty saw Sally Chapman sitting at a fold-up table gluing some newspaper articles into a scrapbook. A cigarette dangled from the left side of her mouth. She's one good-looking babe, Rusty thought — and has a personality to go with it. She'd be even better looking if she didn't smoke.

Sally quickly closed the scrapbook when she saw Rusty walk up. She wore a tight LSU T-shirt with LSU Tiger earrings dangling from her ears.

"What did'cha catch?" She smiled.

"Just a catfish but I released it," Rusty told her.

"Just a catfish?" The smile faded. From the look on Sally's face Rusty wondered if she was recalling something from a distant past.

"Have you ever been hungry, Rusty?" Sally tapped the end of the cigarette.

"Well . . . eh." Rusty patted his stomach. "All the time."

"No, I mean really hungry, going without breakfast, lunch and supper for a day or two."

Rusty saw Sally was serious and the mere thought of going without a meal sent a tremor through his body. "No, ma'm."

"I have." Sally Chapman looked at Rusty and toyed with her left earring. "There was a time when `just a catfish' would have been a delicacy. My father was a bricklayer. He made good money and he played in a country band in a local bar, but almost all his money went to alcohol so my family was so poor that many times we had to rummage through grocery store dumpsters just to get something to eat. When we found a loaf of moldy bread we scraped the mold off and thought we had a treat — especially if it was something multi-grain or rye. Think about it. Mother, my year-old sister and myself, all scrounging for food. Oh, once in awhile we'd go to the soup kitchen or Salvation Army but for the most part we were on our own. And clothes! We did the same thing for clothes. So I made a promise to myself and the moon and stars. I would never, ever be that poor again." She folded her hands and sighed. "I didn't mean to preach to you or tell you how lucky you are because there's what, only five, ten years difference in our ages? Just appreciate what you have." She looked Rusty up and down and crushed the cigarette on the ground. "Oh well, have a nice night." She went into the pop-up.

Rusty walked over to an outside spigot and began to lightly rinse his rod and reel. I'm real hunger, he thought. Here I am with enough . . . He looked at his stomach overlapping his jeans . . . well, more than enough food, yet there are people right here in Florida going hungry. Probably like Sally, going through the dumpsters behind the supermarkets. I can't imagine what it's like to have no food.

Rusty had just turned the spigot off when Wendy barreled out of the RV and grabbed his shirt. "I've got to talk to you. Now!" She pulled him over to a clump of brush. "Those two men waiting for

Bucky McCoy's brother were back at the boat asking Rory and me all kinds of questions."

"Like what?" Rusty walked over to a toolbox attached to the rear of the RV, pulled out a bottle of 3-in-1 oil and applied a few drops to the reel.

"Things like how long Rory and I have worked for Captain McCoy . . . and do we ever go out at night . . . and if so — how far. The only thing is, Captain McCoy's brother wasn't with 'em."

Rusty looked at his cousin with a vacant expression. I'm not about to tell you what happened on the beach, he thought.

"Get this," Wendy continued. "They wanted to know if we'd seen anyone fitting the description of the Chapmans."

"What did you tell them?"

"What d'ya think I told them? What d'ya think is going on?"

Rusty shrugged. "I don't know. I think it's gettin' kind of dangerous. You better not go back."

"Are you nuts? I am going back. This is getting exciting and I'm getting closer to finding the gold — and Rory's taking me out tonight." Wendy got on her bike and pedaled towards the fishing boats.

Now I know something's not right, Rusty thought. Why do I get the feeling danger is lurking somewhere? Oh well. Rusty hung up his rod and reel. As long as Wendy stays away from me, maybe I'll enjoy this vacation.

National Hurricane Center — Florida International University

Inside the concrete fortress of the Hurricane Center, Hurricane Specialist Angie Soto stared at the images sent down from GOES —

Geo Stationary Environmental Satellite. Her stomach tightened as she saw the ugly mass of clouds forming off Mexico near the Yucatan Peninsula. The temperature needed for water to evaporate and start a tropical storm was eighty degrees.

The water in the Gulf of Mexico was eighty-eight degrees at two hundred feet deep, plenty warm enough to stir up the ocean. Off the Yucatan, giant eddies were at ninety degrees at six hundred feet. It was in one of these eddies that this mass of thunderstorms was born.

"What's up, Ang?" Chief Hurricane Specialist Larry Rhodes looked over her shoulder while sipping his coffee.

"Look." Angie pointed to the red blob of rainfall on her monitor. "This isn't right." A similar image lit up a massive map of the tropics on another wall.

"Wonderful. Two depressions off Africa — now this." The good-natured grin was gone along with the last drops of coffee. He looked at the two red masses in the Atlantic slowly churning north, then at the blob in the Gulf, and at the feeder bands swirling above and to the right of the main mass. "I'll get the boss to call Kessler and have them send a recon plane up."

"Those depressions in the Atlantic are supposed to turn away from land. This," Angie grimaced as she tried to explain, "is a gut feeling that's not going to go anywhere but northeast or directly north."

"I appreciate that, Ang." Rhodes looked at the blob as he headed for the door. Can I see the spiral bands and counter-clockwise movement already? Rhodes asked himself. No, it's too soon. Or is it? He looks at some grounds floating in the last drop of coffee. What I need is another cup. He walked out the door.

Deadly Danger

The Parker Campsite — Ft. Pickens Campground

The afternoon thunderstorm had drifted east, leaving hot muggy air behind it. Rusty finished the article on snook in a *Florida Sportsman* magazine and laid it on the bed. His mind wandered. Wendy is with Bucky McCoy, thank God! Mom's taking a nap and it's low tide so fishing won't be that great. I don't dare touch that battery TV Dad brought for emergencies, and there's no computer — thanks to Dad wanting us to get closer. Wendy and I get closer? That's hilarious. Now what? I wonder if Cal's back from town.

Rusty folded and put a clip on what was left of a bag of Cheetos and wrote a quick note to his mother.

He stepped outside and found Noah McCoy talking to the Chapmans. Sally Chapman held a bottle of glue in one hand and a newspaper clipping in the other while Warren Chapman leaned against their aging Nissan pick-up smoking a cigarette. Noah stood downwind from the wafting cigarette smoke.

I didn't realize they knew each other, Rusty thought. He nodded to them and, just as he raised his kickstand he heard Noah say, "I just got out of Marion Correctional two weeks ago. It's hard finding a job when you're an ex-con."

Warren chuckled. "I know where you're coming from. I've been out for two months now and all I can get is a job washing dishes in a greasy spoon. But . . ."

Rusty pretended to check the chain on his bike as he listened.

"If we find that gold, I know someone who'll buy it and we'll never have to work again."

"Sounds sweet," Noah said. "When do we start?"

"We?" Sally looked up from her scrapbook. "How much is there?"

Sally watched Rusty turn the pedals and look at the chain.

"There's enough gold to make the three of us very happy and we've already started looking for it." Chapman lit a cigarette and waved it towards Rusty. "I have that fat kid's cousin getting cozy with that drunken fisherman who claims he knows where the gold is."

Fat kid? Rusty glared at Chapman, thinking, Mister, I didn't like you before now I really can't stand you.

If Noah McCoy resented a stranger calling his brother a drunk he didn't show it. He shrugged and said, "The sooner the better."

Sally played with the LSU earring while she kept her eye on Rusty. "Let's go inside," she said. Sally got up and held the door open for her husband and Noah.

I wonder what she didn't want me to hear, Rusty thought. I've got to tell Cal. Rusty climbed on his bike, took off like the devil himself was after him and pedaled in the direction of the Sapps.

Rusty skidded to a stop in front of Cal Sapp's Ranger house, ignoring sprawling Ft. Pickens that sat a mere quarter of a mile away, and found Cal and his father trimming a large loblolly bay tree. To the right and rear of the house was a pyramid of metal crab traps. Tied to the dock behind the house was a twenty-foot boat with rust marks running down the sides, the midship stacked with rectangular, metal wire crab traps. Rusty recalled Cal saying that his father was a part-time crabber and that sometimes he had to help his dad.

"Noah McCoy said he just got out of prison and Warren Chapman's been out for two months," Rusty panted. "He said there's enough gold to make all three of them very happy."

"They're wastin' their time, Rusty." Mr. Sapp wiped his brow. "There is no gold."

"But Noah McCoy is Bucky McCoy's brother and Bucky McCoy claims he knows where the gold is. They went inside 'cause they didn't want me to hear what they said next."

"Bucky McCoy only says that when he's drunk," Cal added. "but we'll keep our eye on Wendy to make sure she's safe."

"But why bring Wendy in to this?" Rusty asked.

"It sounds like that Chapman fella is slick." Mr. Sapp motioned for Cal to pick up a bundle of branches so he could tie it. "He needs Wendy to do his dirty work."

"But shouldn't Noah know the location of the gold?" Rusty looked at the bundle of branches and, and not wanting to appear as lazy as Wendy, picked up the other end and helped Cal carry the bundle to the curb. "It doesn't make sense. And why do Chapman and Wendy believe there's gold when there isn't any?"

"Some people believe what they want, Rusty, even if the truth hits 'em square in the eye." Mr. Sapp took a long sip of water from a plastic bottle and wiped his mouth off with his sleeve. "Rusty, my buddy is Sheriff, here. I'll have him check this Chapman fella out." Mr. Sapp looked at the loblolly bay tree and the sawed branches. "You boys finish up today and go fishin' tomorrow."

"Yessir!"

The Parker Campsite — Later that Evening

"C'mon, you big lug, and meet my aunt." Wendy pulled on Rory's arm and giggled.

"Not now, baby," Rory said quietly and jerked his arm back.

"Why not?" Wendy whined.

"I gotta go get ready for tomorrow. You do, too."

"Rory!" Wendy pulled on Rory's arm again and almost stumbled.

"Sleep tight, Precious." Rory grabbed Wendy and kissed her hard, then walked into the night.

The sliver of moon played hide and seek with the wooly clouds that concealed the stars. The aroma of burning charcoal wafted towards the boys.

"Gross!" Cal said. "Rory just kissed Wendy on the lips. Where's your mom? She should put a stop to that."

"What?" Rusty looked up from his styrofoam plate containing two massive hamburgers.

Rusty found his mother turning corn-on-the-cob on the grill. He almost laughed when Wendy skipped by singing, "I'm in love. I'm in love for the first time in my life. I'm in love."

Rusty got up to grab a soda and watched Wendy pick up a hot dog bun, a hot dog, a stick and a spoonful of coleslaw, and plopped herself down next to Warren Chapman.

"Hi," she said cheerfully and jabbed the hot dog into the fire.

"Have you found anything?" Chapman placed several dill pickle chips on a hamburger and ran his finger through the mayonnaise on his plate.

"Not yet." Wendy pulled the blackened wiener from the fire and jerked the burnt skin off with her teeth.

"Time is running out." Chapman adjusted the top of his bun.

"What do you mean?"

"I mean other people might find the gold before us. The longer you take, Wendy, the more people Bucky McCoy is going to tell."

Wendy got up. "I'll get the location by tomorrow, Mr. Chapman. I promise."

"See to it." Chapman took a large bite of his hamburger then walked over to his wife who was talking to Rusty's mother.

Wendy's cell phone rang. "Rory! I thought you were going to bed. Oh, you changed your mind." Wendy walked out of hearing range, and soon came back all smiles.

Rusty and Cal sat off by themselves, Cal watching Wendy lean over the table for a salt shaker while Rusty hungrily eyed the hamburgers his mother was flipping. In the background, a classic rock station played a song about a white room with black curtains by a group Rusty never heard of called Cream. It was hard to be heard above the music.

Rusty, now finished with his second hamburger, got up and started for the grill. "Want anything?" he asked. Cal shook his head no.

Rusty came back with a heap of potato salad and a large slice of homemade peach pie Sally had baked. He sat and watched Chapman put his arm around Sally, kissing her cheek then offering her and Diane a Winston. "He's such a liar," Rusty said.

"Who?" Cal asked.

"That Chapman." Rusty shoved a forkful of potato salad into his mouth, chewed and swallowed before answering. "He told me when he first came here he dealt in precious metals. Now, come to find out he's an ex-con and he called me a fat kid. And what about that Rory Abrams?"

Cal shrugged. "Chapman could have dealt in precious metals, made a mistake and wound up in prison. Rory is just plain sorry and lazy. Dropped out of high school, works just long enough to earn money to buy weed. Got caught a couple of times with it. Got off on probation, and . . ." Cal looked around and Rusty knew who he was looking for — Sally Chapman.

"And?" Rusty picked up a potato chip.

"And, Rory's dad's a preacher, one of those hell fire and brimstone kind. A hypocrite, actually."

"What d'ya mean?" Rusty attacked another hamburger.

"One of those 'do what I say not what I do' fellas. He owns a lot of businesses but it's all done kind of shady. Yet he says it's all Christian-like. And he has quite an eye for the women." Cal took a sip of Coke. "Rory just got tired of the double standard so he rebelled."

"We should tell Wendy about him." Rusty scraped his plate for the final remains of salad, held the fork for a minute, while in deep thought, before popping it in his mouth then said, "Nah, she ain't gonna believe me anyway."

Cal got up. "I'll go talk to her."

Rusty frowned when he saw Wendy give Cal an angry look. She jabbed him in the chest, said something to him, then got up and stomped into the RV.

"What happened?" Rusty could see Cal's eyes burning when he returned.

"She accused you of puttin' me up to it. Wendy's lucky she's a girl, Rusty. Nobody pokes me in the chest and gets away with it. Nobody. And also, I smelled tobacco and whiskey on her breath."

"Wow! Now what?" Rusty took a sip of Mountain Dew.

"I gotta think." Cal looked at Rusty in wonder. "Don't you think you should back off, Rusty? I mean that's two hamburgers plus the bread, the massive amount of potato salad and now the pie."

Rusty wiped his mouth. "I'll skip the ice cream."

On the radio the DJ said, "For the rest of the evening, I'm going to be playing double shots of everyone's favorite groups."

He started off with a song about someone to love.

"That's my grandmother's favorite group," Cal said.

"Who?"

"No, the Jefferson Airplane. The "Who" was my aunt's favorite band."

"I could care less about someone to love." Rusty wiped his mouth.

Sally Chapman walked by in short, tight blue and gold shorts, a snug T-shirt with a LSU logo on it, and different Louisiana State earrings. She smiled at the boys, then reached for a bowl of chips Wendy had in her hands as she came out of the RV.

Rusty heard Sally say, "Wendy, if you're not comfortable around Warren, you can tell me the location of the gold. In fact, you can talk to me about anything, anytime, anywhere."

"Thanks. I'm fine," Wendy said. Then proceeded to tell Sally how hot she considered Rory.

"Foxy wife," Cal watched Sally's wiggle as she walked to the table.

"She'd be foxier if she didn't smoke." Rusty finished the burger and took a drink.

"You're right," Cal sighed. "How can a girl turn you on if she smells like smoke? Anyway, we've got to figure out what part Noah McCoy plays in all this. As far as I know, he has a government job doin' something."

Wendy walked by and didn't look at Cal or Rusty.

"So he wasn't in prison?" Rusty wiped his mouth. By this time he was stuffed.

"Not that I know of." Cal still had his eyes on Sally. "Rusty, I got a question."

"Yeah?" Rusty ran his finger around the plate picking up crumbs and drops of ketchup.

"If Sally's married, where's her ring?"

Rusty put his plate down and leaned forward trying to see Sally's left hand.

"Yeah. Yeah! You're right. Be right back." Rusty got up and walked over to the grill pretending to see if there were any burgers left. He walked close to Sally and discovered that she had no wedding band or engagement ring on her left finger.

Rusty came back and slid to the base of the tree. "You're right. No ring."

Cal watched Rusty cut into a pie. "Maybe she has them in the jewelers — getting fixed."

Cal gave Rusty a disgusted glare. "I'm goin' home. We'll take my boat out tomorrow and figure this out."

"Yeah." Rusty popped the last bite of pie into his mouth and got up to for something to drink. As he passed Wendy and Chapman he heard Warren say, "Hound him day and night. Stay on him. You say he drinks?"

"A little. Yes."

"Get him drunk. Anything, Wendy." He pulled out his Winston pack from his shirt sleeve, tapped it then put a cigarette in his mouth.

"How would I do that?" For the first time, Wendy looked a little nervous.

Chapman blew cigarette smoke in Wendy's face. "You're smart. You figure it out."

"Please don't." Wendy made a face and waved the smoke away.

That was it. Rusty hurried over to his mother. "Mom, I need to see you." He looked at Sally Chapman then said, "Alone, please."

Diane gave Rusty a bewildered look and glanced at the remaining hot dogs and burgers on the grill. Sally said she'd look after the food.

Once they were out of ear range, Diane said, "Rusty, you've had two big burgers, potato salad and a big piece of pie. That's enough."

"It's not that, Mom. Mr. Chapman is tellin' Wendy to get Bucky McCoy drunk so she can find out where the gold is."

"What gold?"

"There's a myth that Geronimo hid some gold at Ft. Pickens. It's not true, though."

Diane let out a big sigh then crossed her arms. "Rusty, you watch entirely too much television. That's the most ridiculous thing I have ever heard in my life. You seem not to like Mr. Chapman, and you certainly don't like Wendy, but why make up stories about them? Just leave them alone."

"But it's true, Mom! Cal said she also had cigarettes and booze on her breath."

"She just walked by me and I didn't smell anything. Say good-night and go to bed." Diane huffed off.

Rusty noticed Sally had moved closer to them. What had she heard?

If Wendy had told Mom the same thing about me Mom would have rushed into action, Rusty thought as he brushed his teeth. But no, when I say something, it's brushed off. Rusty changed and climbed into bed. I'm going to have to talk to Dad, he thought. This is too much. Isn't Warren Chapman contributing to the delinquency of a minor? Noah McCoy might want to know. He was concerned about his brother's drinking, but I don't know how to get in touch with Noah. Somehow, someway, I'm gonna right this wrong Mom is doing to me.

A LADY NAMED KATE

The Next Morning — Santa Rosa Island

Rusty rubbed his eyes and looked at Wendy toying with her toast. "Aren't you suppose to be with Bucky McCoy?" he asked.

"That's what's so strange, Rusty."

For gosh sakes! She actually called me Rusty.

Rusty poured a glass of orange juice. "Go on."

"I was supposed to be there at six but when I got there the *SilverKing* wasn't there."

Rusty studied the bubbles in his glass before asking, "Could it have gone for repairs?"

"No. Captain McCoy and Rory do all the repairs themselves."

"Hmm." Rusty drained the glass and hit the sausage and eggs.

"I was trying . . ."

A knock on the RV door interrupted their conversation.

Rusty peeked outside, saw Sally Chapman standing on the metal steps and opened the door.

"Have you seen my husband?" she asked.

Rusty and Wendy both answered in the negative.

"It's strange," Sally said, toying with her earring. "He went out for some cigarettes and never returned."

"I'll get Aunt Diane."

Wendy hurried off. In a minute she was back with Rusty's mother clasping her bathrobe shut with one hand and pushing her hair out of her eyes with the other. "Maybe you should call the sheriff," a sleepy-eyed Diane suggested.

"It's too early," Sally replied. "Oh well, if you see or hear anything please let me know."

All three said they would.

After consuming a stack of pancakes and several sausage patties, Rusty hopped on his bike and headed for Cal's.

So, Warren Chapman went out for cigarettes after the cookout and didn't return. Why? Rusty thought as he biked along. Why would he leave a gorgeous wife and not return? Foul play? Who and why? Man, Rusty shook his head. I'm watching too many CSI shows.

Rusty parked his bike and saw the red-brick Ft. Pickens looming majestically on the horizon. He looked in awe at the top of the fort where a large black Rodman cannon faced the sea. He turned and saw a burned-out section of the fort.

"What happened to that section of the fort?" he asked Cal, who was screwing the gas cap shut on his Carolina Skiff.

"An explosion back in 1899." Cal placed the gas can on the dock. "I'll show you the fort when we get back. Let's go inside for a second."

On the kitchen table of the Sapp's home sat a tall milkshake topped with a large cherry.

"What's that thing?" Rusty stared hungrily at it.

"Don't touch it." Cal picked it up and put it in the freezer. "It's for Wendy."

"Wow! You do care for her."

"Didn't you tell me she likes those milkshakes at the Working

Cow?" Cal grinned slyly at Rusty. "You'll see. C'mon."

Rusty got into the boat. "Good. I need to talk to you out on the water. Oh, and Cal, Sally Chapman came up this mornin' and said her husband was missing."

"Huh?" Cal undid one of the lines and nodded to Rusty. "Grab the other. I wonder what happened."

Rusty wasn't even seated when he heard, "Oh Ca-al, can you show me the fort now? I have to go with Captain McCoy this afternoon, then Rory and I are hanging out. You can come too, if you want."

"No, thanks. So, you're not mad at me anymore?" Cal gave Wendy a skeptical look.

"Oh, last night. I just got upset when I thought fat boy here got to you. I can see you're smarter than that."

"So, it's back to that old routine huh?" Rusty balled his fist. "Stop callin' me names, Wendy!"

The gleam from Wendy's chin ring caught Rusty in the eye. "Besides, I want to see where the gold is."

"There is no gold, Wendy."

Cal looked at Rusty. "Do you mind?"

Rusty turned his hands so his palms faced up. What could he say? Once again Wendy got her way.

National Hurricane Center, FIU — At That Same Time

Everything was in place. The low pressure, the hot water, the moist rising air that becomes unstable and keeps on rising. The storm was far enough from the equator for the 'Coriolis Effect,' the deflection of winds to the right in the Northern Hemisphere caused by the spinning of the Earth, to kick in.

"It's Tropical Depression Number Three now, and it'll be a storm by this evening." Larry Rhodes entered the glass partitions, coffee cup in hand. "Her name is going to be Kate."

"We've seen the computer read outs, Larry." Angie reached for her purse then stood up. "I'm going to lunch. The way that storm is building it's going to be a CAT 5 by tomorrow afternoon."

He nodded. Hurricanes are measured on the Saffir/Simpson scale. A Category One is less severe with winds of seventy-five miles and hour. A Category Five is the worst with winds over one hundred forty miles and hour.

"That's why I'm asking you to stay, Ang." Rhodes looked at the pretty young woman. "You're the best. I wish it was 'overtime' but look at the bright side, once this is over you'll get to spend a few days with Andy."

"This mess is the most remarkable tropical system I have ever seen. It's going to strike somewhere. I want to know where." Angie looked at her watch. "Ray should be getting off of work anytime now, I'll call him and he can take Andy to my mother's."

I'm glad I stocked up on *Lean Cuisine*, Angie thought as she headed for the lounge. For the next few days, no one is going to get much rest around here—thanks to a lady named Kate.

Late Morning at Ft. Pickens — Santa Rosa Island

Wendy, Rusty and Cal entered Ft. Pickens by the visitor's center sally port. Wendy stopped to look at trinkets in the gift shop's window.

"C'mon," Cal urged. "I wanna show you the fort then take my

boat out before the thunderstorms hit."

Leaving the visitor's center, Cal led the cousins into the first chamber to the officers quarters. On the wall facing the outside casemates, gun mounts poked through granite crescents. A fireplace stood on an inner wall. Rusty stared at it, almost feeling the ghosts of the men who once lived there.

Back in the hallway Rusty noticed a lot of arches overhead and he noticed a tunnel. Cal explained that it led to the mine chambers and suggested they travel it. The three had to bend over to proceed down the damp, dimly lit passageway. One mine chamber was on the right just before the corridor ended in a two-pronged fork. Cal told them that each chamber held mines and one thousand pounds of gunpowder. In case the enemy made it to the walls, the mines would be detonated as a last resort.

Rusty had to crab-walk almost back to the main corridor. Panting, he stood up, closed his eyes and stretched. He sprung to attention when he saw three shadows flicker by on the wall.

"See that?" Rusty pointed down the passageway.

"What?" Cal asked.

"Shadows," Wendy said.

"You mean we're being followed?" Cal asked. "C'mon guys, there's at least fifty people waitin' to come in here."

"Those figures moved too quickly." Wendy reached for Cal's hand.

"But why would they be following us?" Cal asked.

"Geronimo's gold," Wendy whispered. "Mr. Chapman was right."

"Whatever." Cal went first. "Let's go."

To the right of the main corridor was a room housing powder magazines. Wood-lined, the interior walls were meant to keep the gunpowder dry. Rusty noticed copper hardware in the magazines. Cal informed him that copper was used because it doesn't spark. Two hundred fifty thousand pounds of black powder was stored in them — enough for two weeks.

"This fort is so big, I wonder how many bricks they used." Rusty looked over his shoulder, trying to pay attention to Cal yet watching their backs.

"Over twenty-one and a half million," Cal answered.

"How interesting." Wendy yawned. "When are we going to find the place where Geronimo stayed?"

"Soon." Cal said.

Past the mine battery room where the mines for the harbor were kept, the passageway ended and blue sky began — the parade grounds. Cal pointed to the southern wall and a closed-in room. "The quarters that used to be there are gone but that's where Geronimo and the Apaches stayed."

"And that's where Geronimo's gold is." Wendy rushed to the outer wall before Cal could get a word out. She looked high and low over each section, then ran her hand across a few salt-encrusted bricks.

"There is no gold, Wendy." Cal looked aggravated. "We're wastin' time."

"It's got to be there." Wendy strolled back to the boys.

"It's not sinkin' in." Cal waved his hand in frustration. "Let's go see the tower and the cannon."

"I think it's interesting," Cal said as the three started up the stairs to the Tower Bastion and the eight-inch Rodman cannon Rusty had seen from a distance.

"What's so important about it?" Rusty asked.

"The man who helped build the fort was the man who fired on it during the Civil War. William Chase was his name. There's the beast."

The huge black cannon sat on a circular railroad trestle and pointed vigilantly out toward the blue Gulf. Rusty looked at the breech, the long barrel, the mechanism that raised it. He closed his eyes and imagined himself ramming a cannonball into the weapon. Rusty snapped back to reality when he heard Wendy say, "Oh no!"

"What's wrong?" Cal asked.

"Those men from the *SilverKing* are here — and Noah McCoy is with them."

"Where?"

"Coming out of the hallway."

Noah spotted the teenagers and pointed them out to the other two. The three men began walking towards them.

"Let's get out of here. This way." Cal led the cousins to a different set of stairs and they scrambled down them to the cistern on the north side of the fort. They began to run. Rusty, being the heaviest, was left behind.

"Wait a minute, Rusty." Noah McCoy shouted to him. "We want to ask you a few more questions."

Rusty ignored him and started running. Puff-puff! I can't let them get me. Huff-huff! And how did he know my name? Wheez! Maybe I should lay off the fried Twinkies. Gasp! Rusty looked over his shoulder and saw no one, then bent over to catch his breath. Maybe I should start exercising. Nah, too hard. Rusty gasped a few more times then ran to Cal and Wendy at the burned out corner of Bastion D.

"My goodness, fat boy, I didn't know you could run." Wendy taunted. "But listen to you."

"Stop it, Wendy." Cal handed Rusty a handkerchief. "We've got more important stuff to think about."

"Yeah," Rusty said in between deep breaths. "Like why were those guys after us."

"You were right." Cal put his hand on Rusty's shoulder. "I reckon we were bein' followed." Cal looked at the sky. "When we get back to the house I think it's time we try to figure out what's goin' on."

Rusty turned and saw the three men, their arms folded, watching them from the Tower Bastion.

A Half Hour Later — The Sapp's Home

"Okay," Cal said over a glass of fresh-squeezed lemonade. "What do we have? Write it down, Rusty." On a sheet of notebook paper, Rusty wrote 'Incidents,' and across from it, he wrote 'Motive.'

"One, Cal paced the kitchen floor, we have Warren Chapman tellin' Wendy to find the location of Geronimo's gold. Then Noah askin' Rusty questions, and two guys askin' you questions, Wendy. Now these same guys are followin' us. Why?"

"They want the gold, too?" Wendy asked.

"But if there's any gold, Noah McCoy should know where it is." Rusty scratched his head. "It doesn't make sense."

"Unless . . ." Wendy looked at the boys. "Noah let Mr. Chapman get the gold then killed him for it."

"We don't know if Chapman is dead. Maybe he just took off. Although why he would leave a beautiful woman like Sally is beyond me."

Wendy scowled at Cal. "He's probably, like, stuffed in a trunk somewhere. He was a such nice guy."

"And Mom says *I* watch too much television," Rusty laughed. "You're too dramatic, Wendy. Noah McCoy told me that Geronimo's gold was a family plague. It sounds like he wants nuthin' to do with the gold, but it seems to me all three of those dudes are capable of murder. And maybe that includes Sally." Rusty looked around the Sapp's kitchen. "Are there any cookies?"

Cal gave Rusty a dirty look. "Forget about your belly for once and think about what's happened. It's too early to think Chapman's missing. He might have stopped at a bar. Noah could be blowin' smoke. So I don't know about the killin' part, Wendy," Cal said. "But a double cross? Could be. Wendy, maybe you should stick close to us." Cal opened the refrigerator for some ice cubes. "Oh, I almost forgot. Here, Wendy." Cal pulled out the milkshake he'd made earlier.

"Oh wow!" Wendy shouted — then frowned. "What's this?"

"A new recipe for a shake," Cal replied. "It's the latest in food fashion. I read about in my mom's magazine."

"Food fashion?" Rusty chuckled.

"What's it made with?" Wendy studied the glass, lifting it so she could see all the way to the bottom.

"Try it and see," Cal winked at Rusty. "I'm sure you'll love it."

Wendy plucked the cherry then dug into the shake. She took one spoonful then gagged. "Ewww! It's horrible. I'm going to be sick." She stuck her tongue out. She rushed to the kitchen sink. "Water!" Wendy cried.

"Here." Cal handed Wendy a glass of lemonade.

Calmed down Wendy said, "your mom needs to read a different magazine, and you're pure evil Cal Sapp." She hurried to the door.

"And furthermore, I'm going to find that gold with or without you." Wendy rushed out into the afternoon sun.

"What was in that shake?" Rusty laughed.

"Besides the cherry? Mashed potatoes covered with molasses for that chocolate effect."

"So, she got a spoonful of very sweet potatoes?" Rusty thought his sides were going to burst.

Cal put his thumb and forefinger to his lips in a chef-like motion. "Mag-ni-fi-cent!"

Both boys laughed until they cried.

Then Rusty looked at the notebook paper and got serious. In the Incident column he wrote: 'Murder, maybe?'

The Parker Campsite — The Next Morning

"I'm fourteen and perfectly capable of making my own decisions."

What's this? Rusty popped one eye open and listened.

"But not wise decisions, Wendy." Rusty's mother said.

"I make informed decisions. I know what I want and know the difference between right and wrong."

"Do you? Do you think drinking and smoking at fourteen is the right thing to do?"

"Oh my god! I did it once to make Rory happy and now I'm being treated like a criminal."

"To make Rory happy? What else have you done 'to make Rory happy?' "

"N o t h i n g!"

"Maybe Rusty's right. You shouldn't hang around with Rory. If anything happens I could never face your mother."

"Aunt Diane, if you don't let me see Rory I'll never speak to you again. You can fly me back to Lakeland. And as for facing my mother, she's never around long enough for anyone to face her."

With that Wendy stamped out of the RV.

My gosh, Mom, Randy thought. He raised his head high enough to see his mother staring out the window. Can you really stand Wendy not speaking to you? You're doing something right. Don't back down. Be strong for once. You're talking about Wendy's life. You're the adult. But . . . you'll cave in like you always do.

The Gulf of Mexico off Pensacola

The Gulf was smooth as a marble counter-top. The tar colored clouds of a thunderstorm hung in the far distance. It looked like Pensacola would be spared the thunderstorms that afternoon.

"This is cool," Rusty said as the Cal's little boat chugged around the tip of Santa Rosa Island.

Cal shrugged. "It's all I can afford right now. I'd like a bigger boat. You know, one with GPS and a fish finder, but Dad says in due time. I'd like to go out further into the Gulf."

Rusty made himself comfortable. "I've never been in the Gulf before, so this is alright."

Cal cruised back towards land and threw the anchor overboard under the shadow of Ft. Pickens. "Grab a soda. There are shiners in the live well or, if you want, there's a white bucktail jig in my tackle box."

Rusty took a small bait fish from the live well, put it on his hook, then castout. "Cal, I want to talk to you. That Chapman told Wendy to get Bucky McCoy drunk."

"Yeah?"

"I mean, we gotta do somethin' to stop it."

"Like what?"

Rusty's pole bent and began shaking. Rusty pulled the pole skyward and started reeling in. "Maybe warn the ol' boy that Warren Chapman is . . . was . . . a bad dude."

"There's something else." Cal cast towards some mangroves.

"What?" Rusty watched the line go left, then right.

"I've never seen Sally and Chapman kiss." Cal reeled in the slack. "You would think maybe just a peck — but never. They put their arms around each other like a couple in love does, but that's it. Take that, and the fact that Sally isn't wearing a ring . . . something isn't right, there.

"You're right, Cal. I only saw them kiss once."

"Who knows? You could warn Bucky, but Rusty, Bucky McCoy's a sailor. He's been on the water his whole life — in the Navy and here. He loves his beer and rum."

"I could ask him not to drink when Wendy's around." Already Rusty's arm ached and he began to tire.

"Give 'em some slack. You could, but it's his boat and he could tell you where to go."

Rusty lowered the pole then raised it again. The fish pulled on the line, struggling for it's freedom, swimming right and left, back and forth, back and forth. "I don't even like Chapman or Rory bein' around Wendy."

"Whoa! Comin' from you that's sayin' something right there."

"I know, I know. But she's still blood." Sweat rolled down Rusty's cheek as he reeled in.

"I'll grab the net."

By the time Cal got the dip net Rusty had the fish close enough to the boat to see the black stripe running length-wise down the silver body. Cal just dipped the net in the water when the fish spit out the hook and swam away.

"Too bad." Cal put the net in its holder. "That was a nice fish."

Rusty put the rod and reel in a rack. "I almost had a snook." He glumly sat down and looked towards the shore. That's the story of my life — almost — and that only counts in horseshoes and hand grenades.

"Hey!" Cal pointed towards shore.

"Yeah?" Rusty mumbled, his chin on his hands.

"Wonder what that black thing is in the water." Cal turned the boat to what looked like a long log floating by the mangroves close to the bank. "I hope it's not a dead dolphin."

"Dead dolphin?" Rusty frowned. Although he never saw a bottlenose dolphin in the wild, Rusty remembered the time he and his parents, without Wendy, went to the Miami Sea Aquarium and watched the Dolphin show. He also liked the old television show *Flipper*.

"I hope not." Cal turned the skiff towards the object. "Occasionally they get tangled up in fishing line."

"That's sad." Rusty turned to look at what his friend was talking about as Cal stopped the engine.

"Oh my god!" Both boys said at the same time as they looked at the swollen, battered body of Warren Chapman floating in the water.

NO ACCIDENT

Santa Rosa Island

"You boys okay?" Mr. Sapp asked Rusty and Cal.

"Yessir," Cal said.

"It's just that I've never seen a dead body before, let alone a murdered one with crabs pecking at it." Rusty wiped his mouth, fighting the nausea that over took him after seeing Chapman's body.

"You didn't touch it, did you?" A husky man in a polo shirt and jeans blew a bubble, popped it, then chomped on the gum. A black pouch with a gold star hung from the man's belt buckle. Rusty could see the well-sculpted muscles beneath the polo shirt.

"No sir, we didn't," Cal said.

Another deputy came up to confer with the man Cal introduced as Sheriff Paul Raymond. The two lawmen stepped out of hearing range.

"What do you think of him?" Cal asked.

"Who?"

"Sheriff Raymond."

"He seems okay."

"That's all?" Cal asked incredulously. "You know who he is?"

"Am I supposed to?"

"Rusty, that's Paul Raymond. He won the Heisman trophy at Florida State and was MVP for the Buffalo Bills in 1995."

"Oh." Rusty said indifferently and continued to watch the crime scene people splash around Chapman's body.

Rusty and Cal joined Mr. Sapp looking for anything unusual on the beach. After a thorough search, they joined Sheriff Raymond just as the medical examiner team put the bag containing Warren Chapman on a stretcher and wheeled him to the van.

"Okay." The sheriff popped his gum. "No signs of gunshots or a knife wound."

"Huh." Cal said.

"However," Sheriff Raymond continued. "There are signs of blunt trauma to head and contusions around the neck. Now, did the trauma come before or after he fell in the bay? That's the question."

"So, someone could have choked him?" Rusty asked, reverting to his television crime shows.

"It's possible." Sheriff Raymond gave Rusty an impressed look.

"Could it have been an accident?" Cal asked. "Like he was drunk and fell?"

"We'll know more when the autopsy is performed and the toxicology report comes back. Right now it doesn't look like it." The lawman's radio crackled. "I gotta go." The sheriff stomped off.

"What do we have, Cal?" Rusty asked as they headed back to Cal's house.

"A dead man that wanted non-existent gold. A gorgeous chick. And Noah McCoy and his buddies."

"I don't think Chapman's death was an accident," Rusty said.

"Neither do I," Cal agreed.

"So, was it someone from Chapman's past? Like, maybe he fingered somebody, they got out and wanted revenge."

"Fingered?" Cal laughed. "You really do stay up late and watch those old detective movies."

"*The Maltese Falcon* is my favorite." Rusty felt his pockets for a Twinkie. Finding none he said, "it sounds like Chapman moved around a bit, so I don't think it was someone from his past."

"So that means it was someone he met here." Cal looked toward Ft. Pickens. "Someone he ticked off?"

"Noah, maybe? Rory?"

"But why?"

Rusty looked at a large clock on the wall of the camp store. It was nearly four o'clock. "Man, I told Mom I'd be home soon. I'll see ya later."

"Rusty!" Cal called. "My dad says we can go fishin' tonight. You wanna go?"

Rusty's face lit up like a Christmas tree. "Yeah! Let me go ask my mom."

"We're leavin' at seven."

"I'll get back with ya." Rusty hurried back to the RV. Fishing at night? Maybe a snook I can throw back. Then his thoughts got serious. Why? Why would someone kill an ex-con? And is Geronimo's gold part of it?

The Parker Campsite

For the first time since he could remember, Rusty Parker was not hungry or thinking about food. The mere thought of seeing fiddler crabs run over Chapman's body, and his lifeless eyes, is enough to make me barf, Rusty thought as he entered the RV. He was relieved to see Wendy sitting at the kitchen table.

Wendy was the one to notice Rusty's pale complexion. "What's wrong Fat . . . er Rusty? Someone steal your Ho-Hos?"

Rusty ignored her and the tuna fish sandwich with his favorite chips, onion and garlic, sitting on the table. In fact, his stomach somersaulted.

"How long have you been here, Wendy?" He asked.

"All morning. What's it to you?"

"Wendy, be nice."

"What's wrong, honey?" his mother said, screwing the mayonnaise lid on the jar.

"Warren Chapman was probably murdered."

Diane almost dropped the jar. "Are you sure?"

Wendy wiped her mouth. "Chub . . . Rusty if you're joking . . ."

"Cal and I found the body." Rusty put both elbows on the table and sank his head into them.

Diane looked out the window at the Chapman's campsite. "I'd better go over and see how Sally's doing. I suppose she knows . . ."

A few minutes later Rusty got up to get a drink, thinking, ain't it funny? Mom didn't even ask me if I'm alright. She goes straight over to the Chapmans. He looked out the window and saw four deputies and several plainclothes officers walking around the Chapman's empty campsite.

Rusty felt Wendy come up next to him, and when he turned to look, he saw that her eyes were watery. The closest she's ever come to crying, he thought.

"I'm still going to find that gold," she sniffed.

"Why?" Rusty watched a plainclothesman pick up a piece of paper.

"I owe it to Warren."

Rusty turned and faced his cousin. "You don't owe him anything.

Did you ever think this . . ." Rusty made the sign of quotation marks with his finger, "gold' is what got him killed in the first place?"

"Doesn't matter. I'm going to tell Rory."

Wendy walked out just as Diane was coming in. "Funny." She poured a cup of coffee. "Sally's missing also. What's going on, Rusty?"

Rusty shrugged. I told you and you wouldn't believe me, he thought. Find out for yourself.

Mark C. Pilles

A BOLT OUT OF THE BLUE

The Gulf of Mexico

"My dad says more and more it's pointing to murder." Cal steered his little boat between the red and green lights on the posts that marked the channel.

"Do they know who did it?" Rusty watched the phosphorescent wake, churned by the boat's propeller, and caused by tiny organisms and fish.

"The sheriff says there's a lot of suspects, including Rory. Plus, get this . . . that Nissan wasn't registered to Chapman. In fact, Chapman couldn't get a driver's license in the State of Florida. Something to do with a DUI and vehicular homicide, so the Nissan and plate were probably stolen." Cal's boat chugged out into open water.

"Wow! He was a bad dude." Rusty reached into his pocket for a snack. "I don't like where this is heading, Cal."

"Why? There's an artificial reef just ahead about mile."

"Not that. Chapman. Chapman and Wendy. Maybe Rory.

You're right." Cal bit into an ice cube. "We're going to have to keep a close eye on Wendy— a very close eye."

The sun had gone down in a conflagration of reds and yellows. The lights of Pensacola cast a pale glow into the sky. Stars flickered overhead as Cal eased the little boat over the artificial reef which once saw action as a navy cargo ship and was now home and a buffet to a myriad of marine life. He shut the motor off and dropped the anchor overboard. The moon, a thin crescent, hung low in the eastern sky. Cal bent over for his pole. "We should catch some grouper, definitely some trout and possibly a tarpon."

"Tarpon?"

"Yeah, and buddy you better hang on. Grab a shrimp or some cut bait."

"I'd like to catch a snook." Rusty cast out and began to wait. "You go fishin' a lot, Cal?"

Cal cut a pinfish into quarters then placed a piece on his hook. "Not as much as I'd like. Mom has a bad heart so I help her as much as I can. Since this is summer, Dad says I should enjoy bein' a kid 'cause in a few short years I'll have a job and that will be it."

The boys cast out, Rusty on the starboard side, Cal on the port. After a couple of minutes, Rusty felt a tug on his hook. He set it but, as usual, whatever it was spit the hook out.

"I've got something!" Cal set the hook and began reeling in. "Whatever it is, it's a fighter." Cal lowered then raised his rod. After a few minutes he reeled in a nice-size Spanish mackerel. Rusty could barely make out the green back and yellow spots as Cal shined his flashlight on the fish. He removed the hook and threw the fish overboard.

"You can eat 'em but I want something better." Cal baited his hook again.

Maybe I should try some cut bait, Rusty thought and put a piece of the cut pinfish on his hook then cast out. He waited, his mind filled with thoughts of what he would catch. Warren Chapman's body and — why did she have to enter my thoughts — Wendy.

Then, in the dark of night, a very large silhouette appeared in the distance. It stayed off the coast in deeper water. Boy, it looks like one of those cargo ships I've seen in the movies, Rusty thought. No running lights showed and it flashed a green light only once. A white light flashed once in return and Rusty noticed a smaller boat heading out to it.

"Cal, what's that?" Rusty pointed to the two boats.

"Lower your voice. I dunno." Cal put his fishing pole down and watched the two boats. "Hmmm, could be smugglers."

"Smugglers!" Rusty gasped. "What would they be smuggling?

"Drugs most likely."

Suddenly the sky and water lit up like daylight and the boys were caught in the spotlight's beam. A voice shouted in Spanish. Then the boys felt something whiz by above their heads and heard the sound of gunfire.

"Let's go!" Cal pulled the cord on the engine, which sputtered to life. He turned his boat towards shore — motor at full throttle.

Rusty looked back at the two boats and saw the larger one lower, not one, but two rubber Zodiacs into the Gulf. They began to move toward Cal's boat. "They're after us, Cal," Rusty yelled.

"Let them," Cal shouted back, turning the throttle to forward. "I know these waters like the back of my hand."

Rusty watched one Zodiac cruise over the calm water and close in on them. "They're gainin' on us!" he yelled. Cal was too busy, steering and concentrating on what lay ahead, to look back.

The large spotlight from the ship kept following the boys.

"I wonder where the other Zodiac is?" Rusty shouted. The thunder of the engine and the wind pounded in Rusty's head. "If there was some way to knock that light out . . ."

"Who knows? Holy . . . !" Cal ducked as another bullet whizzed by him. He began to zig-zag in an effort to throw off the shooter's aim, but the Zodiac was quickly approaching Cal's small craft.

"They're almost on us," Rusty cried.

"Okay, Rusty. Hang on tight."

Suddenly Cal spun the little boat around and headed right for the Zodiac. Caught off guard, the shooters stopped for a moment. Within twenty feet of the Zodiac, Cal turned again, the heavy wake bouncing one of the shooters into the water.

Cal turned towards home. "That was close." he said, wiping the sweat from his forehead.

"Too close," Rusty sighed with relief.

Then, just as Cal and Rusty were calming down, the second Zodiac appeared in front of them.

"Darn it," Cal shouted and turned the throttle full speed.

The men in the second Zodiac weren't shooting. "Maybe they want us alive," Rusty yelled.

"This is gonna be close," Cal warned.

Still moving at full speed, Cal brought his boat through the channel and hugged the shoreline in water just deep enough not to go aground.

"Hold on!" Cal shut the engine off and jumped out of the boat.

"What are you doin'?" Rusty asked — horrified.

"Jump out and be quick. Get behind the boat and push. I'll pull from the bow."

Rusty did as he was told and although Rusty grunted and groaned a lot, in thirty seconds the boys had the boat across a sandbar. After they ran the boat ashore, Cal pointed to a clump of sea oats. He motioned for Rusty to get down and the two of them watched the Zodiac speed towards the shore. Rusty tightened up when he saw the machine guns glimmering in the spotlight.

"They mean business, Cal," Rusty whispered.

"So do we," Cal replied. "Watch."

The bow of the Zodiac was in the air, the watercraft cruising at a high rate of speed. Unaware of the submerged danger, the Zodiac hit the sandbar and flipped end over end.

The boys heard the curses in English and Spanish, saw the flashlights shine along the shore. The men up-righted the Zodiac and with damage to the motor, rowed back to the mother ship.

"That was a close one, Cal. Those guys were serious."

"Big time. We'll row home."

"Row?" Rusty gave Cal an uncertain look.

"Yeah. It's only about a half mile."

"A half mile," Rusty groaned. "Did you get a close look at any of those guys?" Rusty took a long stroke with the oar, hoping their talking would keep his mind off the hard work of paddling.

"No, it was too dark. And those two boats came like a bolt out of the blue."

After the boys made it to the Sapps, they sat on the dock, feet dangling over the side.

"Why were they chasing and shooting at us, Cal?" Rusty looked out into the Gulf. "I was scared."

"Now, that it's over, I'm shaking. My guess is, they definitely were smugglers."

"Wonder what they were smuggling?" Rusty jumped as a mullet leaped out and back into the water with a splash.

"Like I said, probably drugs."

"And they would kill someone over that?"

Cal shrugged.

It hit Rusty like a slap in the face. "Cal, didn't that smaller boat bear a strange resemblance to the *SilverKing*?"

Cal looked at the starlit sky. It seemed so quiet, eerily quiet now that the shooting was over. "Now that you mention it . . ." He got up. "We better tell my dad."

Mr. Sapp sat in his recliner with a bag of pretzels and a can of root beer by his side watching a Miami Marlins/San Francisco Giants' baseball game being played in San Francisco. He clicked the remote to mute and listened to the boys.

The story spilled out of them almost without a pause. Mr. Sapp got up from his chair. "Are you sure they were shooting at you?"

Both boys shook their heads. "It sounded like it to me, Dad," Cal said."

"But they didn't hit the boat or the two of you? Guess they were just tryin' to scare you off.

"Boys, what you say confirms the rumors that've been floatin' around here. I'll call the Sheriff, right now. He's probably gonna want to talk to you. Just go about your normal business, but Cal, you two keep away from those marinas. Hear?"

Normal? Rusty thought. What was normal about this last week?

DEADLY DANGER

The Next Morning at the Parker Campsite

Rusty hungrily eyed the last piece of bacon on the plate. It wasn't that he was hungry. He'd just finished three eggs, five pancakes and six pieces of bacon. His mother warily eyed the television screen, watching the counter-clockwise, red semi-circle and the white dot in the middle of the Gulf.

That last piece should do the trick, Rusty thought. He reached for the strip of bacon — but Wendy beat him to it.

Rusty finished his orange juice and put the glass in the sink. "I'll think I'll go with you to Captain McCoy's, cousin.

"I want to ask him about takin' me out for a snook. It's as good excuse as any for looking around the boat."

Diane turned from the television and picked up the empty pitcher. "That hurricane looks like it's turning away from here. Wendy, how is it working with Captain McCoy? You haven't said. All you talk about is Rory."

"It's good. The only thing is Captain McCoy won't let me go below. I don't know why. Every time I get near the door, Rory or the Captain is there. I'm only allowed in the galley and on deck."

Diane refilled Rusty's juice glass.

"Maybe he'll come around."

Wendy bit off a piece of the bacon. "Why do you want to come with me, Rusty? But you won't be staying?" Wendy's eyes pleaded.

"Nah, I've got stuff to do."

"Maybe you should, Rusty." Diane shut the TV off and picked up a dish cloth. "I'm sure Wendy could use a hand."

"No!" Wendy shouted. Seeing her Aunt's alram, she said sweetly, "Please!"

"Alright, Wendy, if you insist." Rusty's mother put a cup away.

There it was, again. 'If you insist.' Wendy is always the boss over Mom though Mom's the adult. And just as I thought, Mom caved in. She's even letting Wendy see Rory.

"Good." Wendy got up. "See ya there, Tub a . . . a, Rusty. Oh, and Aunt Diane, I'm bringing Rory home with me so you can meet him."

"Fabulous. I'm anxious to meet him."

"You heard what she was about to call me, didn't you?" Rusty asked when Wendy was out of hearing range.

"I'm sure she was just teasing, honey."

"She wasn't, Mom. She does it all the time. And even if she was teasing, it still hurts."

"You know that old saying, 'sticks and stones can break my bones but names can never hurt me.' "

Rusty slammed his juice glass down causing Diane to jump, then pushed his plate away and got up. "That's a crock and you know it. I'll be back in a half hour." Rusty had his hand on the door. "Oh and Rory? He's a grown man and a creep. And what have you done about her smoking and drinking?"

Something needs to be done, Rusty thought on the way to Bucky McCoy's. I can't take the next five years of my mother taking Wendy's side. And what if smoking and drinking's not all Wendy does to please Rory. How about marijuana, or crack? And . . . and just suppose Wendy gets . . . Who's gonna raise the kid? Aunt Susan? Heck no! Wendy? I doubt it. I know, I know — Uncle Jerry and Aunt Diane — with Cousin Rusty to babysit in a pinch. I need to call Dad.

Rusty pulled out his cell phone and punched his father's number. He got his dad's voice mail. He left a message that he'd call back.

Rusty decided to ride over to the Sapps before heading to the *SilverKing*. He wondered if they'd heard anything about Chapman's autopsy, and what Cal was doing later in the day.

He gave the kickstand a tap and turned his bike towards the Ranger House. He looked at the Chapman's deserted campsite. She hasn't been seen since yesterday morning? Why not? Did she kill her husband? Why? So she and Noah could keep the gold? Rusty shivered. She seemed so nice.

A commotion caught Rusty's ear as he eased his bike to a stop in the Sapp's driveway. He looked at the open garage just as a heap of yard tools crashed to the concrete.

"Darn it." Cal rubbed his forehead. "I told my sister to hang them up."

Cal laid a gas lawn edger against the garage wall.

"Whad'cha find out?" Rusty asked.

"No word yet," Cal pulled a lawn mower out onto the scrubby lawn.

"Do you think we should tell Sheriff . . . what's his name . . ."

"Raymond."

"Yeah, Sheriff Raymond — about the gold?"

Cal grabbed a rake and hung it on a hook. "He's probably heard about it. But I guess any info we have, he could use. Who knows?"

Cal looked around the yard. "I can't do anything now. I gotta mow and weed. Maybe tomorrow we can do something."

"See ya."

I don't believe it. It seems all Cal does is yard work. I'd die if I had to work that hard. Thank god Dad hired a lawn-mowing service. It's bad enough that I have to clean my room and do the dishes . . . sometimes. Rusty grit his teeth. Or like all the time on this stupid vacation.

He arrived at the *SilverKing* only to find a half-empty case of Budweiser between Wendy and Bucky McCoy. Norma Jean had her beak open while the old fishing guide poured a bottle of the amber liquid into it.

Wendy didn't see Rusty climb aboard. She twisted a bottle cap, took a sip, eased closer and handed the bottle to the old fishing guide.

"Thankee. Here Norma Jean."

"But like what wall, Captain McCoy?" Wendy smiled.

Bucky McCoy took a long swallow on the beer, gave the pelican the rest then tossed the bottle onto the deck. "My great-granddaddy said the south wall, about a third of the way up. Hold on, Norma Jean."

"A third of the way up, hmmm . . .?" Wendy grinned wickedly. "That'll do it."

The pelican tapped the old fishing guide's arm wanting more beer. Wendy reached into the case and pulled out another bottle then twisted the cap. "Last one, Norma Jean."

"What are you doin', Wendy?" Rusty asked in horror.

"What does it look like?"

"You shouldn't be drinkin' beer."

"I just took one sip, you dweeb."

"He man! You're turnin' her into an 'alky'. How many did *she* have?" Rusty nodded to the wobbling pelican. "You might kill her."

"This is the fourth. And ye ain't gonna kill her. Ye should see her drink scotch." Bucky McCoy burped. "What do ye want, boy?"

"Well, I'd like to talk to you about catchin' snook."

"Snook? Why snook? Grouper, now that's a fighter. Why, one time a grouper pulled me overboard and I had to fist fight him for twenty minutes."

"Awesome, Captain McCoy. But like how do I get to it?" Wendy asked.

So, while Wendy plied Bucky McCoy with beer and questions, Rusty quietly slipped along the starboard railing to the cabin. He slowly turned the doorknob and was about to enter when he heard, "Hey darlin'." Rory leaped onto the deck from the dock then froze in his tracks when he saw Wendy. "Hey, what're you doin'?"

"I'm getting so tired of people asking me that." Wendy took a sip of beer. "I just got the exact location of the gold."

"But getting him and the bird drunk isn't the way to do it. The beer — you didn't go below for it, did you?" Rory gave Wendy a scorching look.

"No, Rory, I didn't. I found it in the galley." A sudden sadness swept over her. She looked at the first mate with something between adoration and despair.

Rory walked over to Wendy. "Something wrong?"

"Rory, Warren Chapman is dead and the police think he's been murdered."

"You're joking, right." Rory sat on the live well and lit a cigarette. "And Sally, is she okay?"

"She's missing." Rusty chimed in.

"Darn." Rory shook his head and blew a puff of smoke. "That Chapman was a good guy."

"I know," Wendy sniffed.

"Now." Rory tossed his cigarette overboard. "About these guys."

"Geronimo's gold, Rory." Rusty waved at Wendy. "Chapman put her up to it."

"Shut up, Rusty!" Wendy spit.

"Chill out, both of you. Cap'n?" Rory knelt over the sleeping fishing guide. "He's buzzed."

Just then Norma Jean let out a loud belch and dropped like a stone next to the Captain.

Rory nodded towards the pelican. "And her. It's a wonder she's not dead." He bent and felt Norma Jean's neck.

Suddenly Wendy looked scared. "Is . . . is she okay? Captain McCoy said we couldn't kill her. She likes scotch."

"She's breathing. I've never seen the man give her booze." Rory shook his head and snickered. "I've never heard of a pelican with a hangover." He looked at Wendy. "Excuse us, Rusty." He took Wendy's arm and led her to the stern, his hand going lower and lower down Wendy's back. He pointed to the mainland then put both arms around Wendy. He held her tight — and they kissed.

"I've seen and heard enough," Rusty said to no one. He moved towards the gangway and took another look at the captain and the pelican. Norma Jean, he thought, there's no way I can sober you up. You're gonna hafta sleep it off.

Wendy came back smiling, skipping over the beer bottles and hurried to her bike. "We've got the location," she shouted. "We're out of here."

"You okay?" Rory called to Rusty. He walked over and put his hand on Rusty's shoulder.

Rusty moved away. "Yeah. I'm goin'."

Rusty took one more look at Norma Jean and Bucky McCoy and shook his head. You've no idea of what you just did, Captain. No idea at all.

The Parker Campsite — Evening of the Same Day

Rusty had his fishing pole in one hand and the bait bucket with an aerator in the other hand, and was returning to the campsite when he saw Noah McCoy and Rory talking at the Chapman's vacant campsite.

"So, she checked out." Rusty heard the anger in Rory's voice. "She sure as hell surprised me."

Noah had his left foot on a mound of shell and chewed on a toothpick. "We better lay low. By that I mean she's as guilty as sin and The Man will have an APB out for her but he'll still want to question us. And we can't risk anything right now."

Rory gave Noah a mocking look. "You're right. Your brother and I have a charter tonight. We should be back first thing in the morning." Rory threw a cigarette butt on the ground and crushed it with his left foot.

"Do you have to?" Noah switched sides with the toothpick. "The net is tightening."

Rusty quickly and quietly stepped over to another campsite close to the Chapmans and knelt behind an old blue and orange Volkswagen van with peace signs and flowers painted on it. The acrid smell of marijuana and the music of the Grateful Dead permeated the air.

"This should be the last. One more — if I change my mind."

"It better be." Noah scanned the area. "We're just going to have to continue without her. If caught, we plead dumb."

"The only thing that concerns me is the girl, Noah." Rory pulled a pack of Camels from his shirt pocket. "She's so hung up on me, and that Geronimo's gold thing, it's sad."

"She's a problem. But the fat kid is a bigger one." Noah ran his hands through his hair. "The sooner we do something about them the better. That girl is bound and determined to find the gold. The fat, freckled faced kid? I don't know."

Rusty clutched the rear bumper of the VW as a vise-like hand of fear clutched his chest. *Fat? Freckled face? I'm getting so sick of grown-ups calling me fat behind my back. Run? Net tightening? I knew Rory was no good. But Noah? Jeez.* Rusty shuddered and stood up. *We're in danger — deadly danger.*

BATTLE LINES

It made perfect sense. The *SilverKing* gone at night, Wendy not being allowed below. Were Bucky McCoy and Rory afraid of what she would find? Cal didn't think it was the old fishing guide's boat. "Proof," he'd said. "We need proof."

Rusty didn't want to go to the RV just yet. Who can I tell? Who is going to believe me? He sauntered down the shell and quartz road. The Sapps are in Pensacola, and Mom definitely won't believe me. I'll have to keep my eye on Wendy and those guys until I can talk to Mr. Sapp.

Rusty strolled back to the campsite — lost in thought. I wish I could have heard what they were planning to do with the gold — if there is any. And more and more it looks like there is.

Rory and Wendy were at the campsite. Rusty saw her leaning on the driver's side window of a metallic-green, low rider Toyota pick-up. The metal flakes sparkled in the noon-day sun.

Rusty rolled his eyes. Great. Just great.

He heard his cousin laugh and say, "C'mon, you big dummy." Wendy pulled on Rory's arm while he got out of the pick-up. She had a big grin on her face, and held Rory's hand as they walked up to the RV.

This is worse than I expected, Rusty thought, eyeing the box of chocolates in Rory's hand. They're probably for Mom and Mom is gonna get suckered in.

Rusty stopped on the quartz road and watched Rory bow, offering Diane a large box of candy. He watched his mother's expression go all aflutter. "Why thank you, Rory. It's been a long time since a man gave me chocolates."

Rory bowed again.

"My pleasure ma'm. Sweets for a lovely lady."

Diane tittered again.

Shoot, I wish Dad was here. But I'm afraid it's gone too far for even Dad to do anything to stop this runaway train.

Rory didn't go into the RV but he and Wendy sat outside by the fireless camp-fire ring.

Unseen, Rusty crouched by the rear bumper of the RV and listened.

"Maybe this afternoon we'll go down and look at rings." Rory ~~put his arm~~ around Wendy.

"Rory, do you mean it?" She looked at Rory with adoration.

"You bet."

"But I'm only fourteen . . . "

"It don't matter. In Las Vegas everything's different."

"Las Vegas?" Wendy asked. "I thought we were goin' to New Orleans. What about my mother?"

"I changed my mind. Besides, it sounds like she don't care for you one way or the other."

Wendy looked at the ground. "True."

No! Rusty thought. If things were out of control before, they were in a total tailspin now.

Deadly Danger

National Hurricane Center — FIU

The pre-existing winds blew in the same direction as the surface wind, converging and sucking up cold water from the bottom of the Gulf. Air so unstable rose at an incredible rate. Humid air above the turmoil was pulled into the storm as extra water vapor provided more energy.

The permanent grin on Larry Rhode's face was gone due to two tropical depressions in the Atlantic, Tropical Storm Kate and his empty coffee cup.

"The recon plane says the pressure is dropping super fast. The eyewall is building and the winds increasing. We're putting out a Hurricane Warning from Marco Island to the Big Bend area near Quincy. From Quincy to Biloxi, there's a Hurricane Watch."

Issuing warnings is never an easy job. At best, the warnings save thousands of lives, at worst, if a storm misses an area under a warning, businesses lose thousands of dollars due to closings. But raised in Miami, then a stint in the Air Force as a weatherman, Rhodes had seen first hand what a major hurricane can do and was satisfied that he was helping people all he could.

"I've never seen a storm grow so fast." Angie watched the feeder bands grow tighter around the counterclockwise swirl.

"The Gulf is the warmest it's been in years, plus the wind shear we hoped for is gone." For the next few days, almost every person who lives along America's gulf coast would keep ears glued to the radio or eyes glued to the television to see where Kate would come calling."

The Parker Campsite

"Fat Boy, wake up." Wendy whispered and shook her cousin's shoulder.

"Leave me alone. The sun hasn't even risen." Rusty rolled over.

"Listen geek, and listen well. Remember that porn site you went to? The one where they're doing all that kinky stuff?"

Rusty had both eyes open now. "It was a accident. I was in a hurry and pushed the wrong keys."

"And how about that *Playboy* under your bed? The one Aunt Diane doesn't know you have"

"Wendy, what are you doing up this early?" Diane asked sleepily.

"I'm just telling Rusty about me going with Captain McCoy today, Aunt Diane."

"Oh. Have a lovely time." Diane rolled over and went back to sleep.

"I wanted to read the interviews in them." Rusty, fully awake now, sat up and rubbed sleep out of his eyes. "I know where you're goin' with this, Wendy."

"Can't you two whisper?" Diane asked.

"Sorry, Aunt Diane."

Wendy lowered her voice. "Yeah, well. Rory and me are like going after the gold this morning and when we find it, we're going to New Orleans. If anyone finds us I'll know you ratted on us and I'll call Aunt Diane about that website and the magazines. She'll flip out and think you're a perv and want counseling for you." Wendy had her back to Rusty then turned around. "I'm out of here and remember — not a word."

"You and Rory goin' to New Orleans? That's funny."

"What's so funny about it, Fatso? We're getting married."

"Yeah? And what makes you think Rory is gonna stick around?"

"He loves me."

Rusty surpassed a grin. "Okay. And how do you plan to get sell the 'gold' if and when you find it?"

"That's up to Rory. Like I've got the exact location and Rory's off today, so . . . " Wendy edged towards the door.

"Wait!"

"Ahhh, coming to your senses, eh, fat boy?"

Dianc moaned.

"Wendy! Talk lower, please." Diane moaned.

"No. Listen to me. I was comin' back from fishin' yesterday when I heard Rory and Noah McCoy talkin'."

"Yeah? So?"

"They want to kill us because we know too much."

Wendy rolled her eyes and let out a deep sigh. "Chubby, you get more stupid every second! Those guys are like our friends. They're not going to kill us. I'm outta here."

"Have a good life, Wendy."

Rusty sat on the edge of the bed, yawned and thought. It was a heck of way to wake up. Wendy is right. If Mom finds out she'll go ballistic. Dad might chalk it up to curiosity, but not Mom. Shoot, Mom wears those long baggy shorts down to her knees and her bathing suits are something out of the forties. Now what? Anyway you look at it, I'm screwed.

Mark C. Pilles

Aboard the WC-130 Hurricane Hunter Aircraft #771

"This should be a goody." Air Force Reserve Captain Tom Conway looked down at the calm waters of the Gulf of Mexico.

"As long as we get back in time for the Brave's game." Co-pilot Joe Flynn took a sip of coffee.

"Why don't you be a fan of a real team — like the Cubs?" Navigator Sean O'Toole radioed up.

"Are you kiddin'? Atlanta's goin' to the Series this year."

"Ha! And a pig is gonna fly, too."

"Are you guys gonna come see me play in the Roy Hobbs game tomorrow?" Flynn asked.

"Yeah," Weather Officer Demetrius Miller chuckled. "We can always use a good laugh."

The modified Lockheed C-130 Hercules was forty-five minutes away from Hurricane Kate. The weather and Gulf looked placid. Weather Officer Miller went over the instruments one more time. Two other officers made up the 'Herks' remaining crew: Flight Engineer David Woodruff and the Dropsonde Officer Kyle Eldridge. The Dropsonde Officer was in charge of dropping the dropsondes-cylindrical tubes that floated to the surface measuring temperature, barometric pressure, humidity and wind speed of a hurricane into the roughest of hurricanes. The only modifications were state of the art weather computers and two extra fuel tanks installed in the cargo area — enough for an eleven-hour trip. The C-130 and crew were members of the 53rd Weather Reconnaissance Squadron out of Kessler Air Force Base near Biloxi, Mississippi.

The easy banter of the crew ended when O'Toole radioed, "I've got her on radar!"

Deadly Danger

Kate was less than twenty miles away. Conway ordered the crew to buckle up. The rodeo ride was about to begin.

A light rain fell on the windshield, becoming harder and harder, and soon turning into a squall. Weather Officer Miller started collecting High Density Data which he relayed to the National Hurricane Center every thirty seconds.

"The eyewall is just ahead," O'Toole radioed.

"Finished your coffee?" Conway asked.

"Just in time," Flynn answered as the first turbulence hit the plane.

Kate picked the airplane up then let it fall like a yo-yo, up and down, up and down, shaking it as hard as shaking a spray can of paint. Conway held the wheel in an iron-fist grip trying to see through the blend of rain and clouds loaded with moisture.

In the cargo area, while Elridge prepared the dropsondes, Flight Engineer Woodruff made sure the Herk was okay after the battering it was receiving. Outside, the crew saw white clouds, dirty white clouds, clouds stacking up on one another — building to a height of fifty thousand feet, clouds so thick the crew could not see anything below.

"Look at the wings!" Woodruff radioed.

The men looked out the window. The wings were flapping ever so slightly, but enough to show how powerful Kate was. Then all was calm. The sun shined on the tower of clouds and below, through a small circle, the crew could see the sparkling Gulf of Mexico; the Herk had flown into the eye of the storm.

"Here's the center," O'Toole radioed. "Dropsondes away."

"Got it." The crew watched the two-foot long cylinders head for Gulf and the parachutes unfurl on top of them. Miller fervently typed information on one of his computers and sent it to a satellite, which would transmit it to the Hurricane Center. Miller paused and took a long look at the screen. “They’re not going to like this, gentlemen.”

“Why?” Conway asked.

“This lady is on the move and growing fast.”

“Let’s take one more spin and do some sightseeing,” Conway said, and turned the aircraft into the second half of Kate.

The Hurricane Hunter flew in three directions and dropped more dropsondes so Miller could send information on the storm from all four points of the compass.

Halfway through the final pass the crew heard a loud explosion followed by a rap-rap-rap on the fuselage behind the left wing.

“The radio antenna’s gone,” Woodruff called.

“Will it wrap around the propellers?” Flynn asked.

“We’ll keep our eye on it,” Woodruff answered.

“Great,” Flynn moaned. “Now we’ll have to listen to this all the way home.”

“Unless you want to get out and cut it,” Conway smiled.

“No thanks.”

From the cockpit the men saw the thick, black dangling cable slap the side of the airplane just short of the engines. It would be a tricky job, but both Connelly and Flynn had experience flying crippled aircraft in the Persian Gulf. The Herk flew out of the storm into calmer skies then headed for home and a baseball game.

National Hurricane Center — FIU

In Monterey, California, at the U.S. Navy Fleet Numerical, the Cray C90 Supercomputer and it’s counterpart in Chevy Chase,

Maryland, spewed out numbers and information and shared it with the National Hurricane Center.

Kate, just a tropical storm a day before, was now a full fledged Category 3 Hurricane with winds of one hundred twenty-five miles an hour and increasing. Angie Soto looked at the map. The Gulf of Mexico could barely be seen beneath the storm. Angie called Larry Rhodes, "Good news, Larry. Kate is moving towards a sparsely populated part of Mexico."

"That's the best news I've heard all week." Rhodes grinned, lifted his coffee cup in a toast then drained it. "I'm going to buy you the best cappuccino there is."

"Expresso," Angie grinned back. "Several of them."

A collective sigh went up from the people along the U.S. gulf coast as they watched Kate turned toward Mexico.

The Parker's Campsite — Later the Same Day

"Ms. Chapman!" Rusty walked over to the battered Nissan. "Where've you been? Everybody's lookin' for you."

"I've been . . . ah . . ." The new widow looked around. "Busy."

"We thought you might have skipped town."

Even though the sun was at tree top level, Rusty wiped the sweat from his brow and saw Wendy lower a large cardboard box.

"I thought you were with Rory."

"What a dweeb. We needed some extra tools." Wendy sneered as she put a trowel in the box.

Sally finally found her voice, "No Rusty, I didn't skip town. I've been around. Wendy, there's not much time." Sally leaned against the driver's door of the Nissan.

"What do you mean?" Wendy asked

"I'm leaving tomorrow — gold or no gold. This hurricane's got me spooked."

"Like, how can you leave? Your husband may have been murdered. And like, I've found the exact spot . . . and Rory and me are going after it right now," Wendy said. "Besides, my aunt said the hurricane is moving away from here."

"I've given the police my cell-phone number, plus where they can find me."

"Where are you going?"

Sally stopped and toyed with her LSU earring. "Home, Wendy. Home to Louisiana."

"But the gold," Wendy whined.

"How can you say you're going after it now? It's been close to a week." Sally gave Wendy a wary look. "You and Rory aren't holding out on me, are you?"

"Why would we do that?"

The newly widowed woman opened the truck door and studied Wendy before getting in. "I don't know, Wendy. Why would you do that? You know you're going to have to split your share with Rory, don't you?"

Wendy nodded.

Rusty stepped into the campsite. "She can't hold out on you, Mrs. Chapman because there is no gold."

"Shut up, you geek!" Wendy hissed.

"Everyone that works at Ft. Pickens says there's no gold."

"No Rusty, Warren did a lot of research," Sally said quietly. "There *is* gold at Ft. Pickens. Perhaps even some off the coast."

"See? I told you, you nerd," Wendy squeaked.

"Eat me, zit farm!"

"Steven Walter Parker!" Diane had been talking to a new family that had just arrived from Orlando.

"I've had enough." Rusty got up and went into the RV and watched Sally pull away and Wendy standing by her bicycle with the cardboard box in her arms. Diane followed him in.

"Why do you always have to pick on your cousin?" she asked. "I'm getting sick of it, Rusty. Every time I turn around you're calling her names.

"I don't, Mom. Why do you always have to take her side?"

"I don't. It's just . . ."

"Don't tell me about how messed up Wendy's life has been. I'm sick of hearin' it. You hear what you want to hear, Mom, and believe what you want to believe, even — if it's not the truth. You stood right here and heard Wendy call me a tub-of-lard and fat boy And you did not say one word to her. Yet if I say something to her, I get in trouble."

"How can you say that? You're my son and I love you."

"You love me only until Wendy comes around. Then you take her side on everything. You do it so much you don't even know you're doin' it, Mom."

"You don't understand, Rusty."

"You're right, I don't understand. Maybe you should explain it to me."

"Not now. Some other time." Diane held her arms out to her son.

Rusty ignored her attempt at reconciliation. "Is she the daughter you never could have?"

"What?" Diane dropped her arms.

"You're always tellin' people you wanted a daughter but never could have one after your last miscarriage. Is Wendy the substitute?"

"Rusty. That hurts. Besides, it's so absurd it's not funny."

"You're right, it's not funny." Rusty turned towards the bathroom and opened the door. "And another thing, why are you letting a grown man hang around with a girl who's not even in high school?"

"It's just he's so charming and . . . and good for Wendy."

"Good like a snakebite. And for your information, Wendy is planning to run off with Rory to New Orleans. She also followed Chapman's advice and got Bucky McCoy and his pelican drunk — not to mention drinking some beer herself. Listen to yourself, Mom. Speak of the devil." Rusty heard the pick-up pull up, looked out the window and saw Rory kiss Wendy as she got in on the passenger side. The two rode off in a veil of dust.

Rusty saw his mother's eyes and saw her tremble just a little bit. Diane had watched the whole scene unfold between Wendy and Rory.

"Think about what I told you, Mom," Rusty said before stepping into the sunlight.

Instead of heading towards Pensacola Beach, Rusty headed towards the tip of Santa Rosa Island. Now it's out. Battle lines are drawn. Mom knows how I feel. Rusty kicked a shell. She knows that I know Wendy is first in her life. Good gosh! How could she? She carried me for nine months. He picked up a stick and hurled it towards the Gulf.

For the rest of that afternoon and evening Rusty didn't speak to his mother, not even when Wendy failed to show up. It's up to Mom now. As the old saying goes, 'let the chips fall . . .'

GOOD 'N DEAD

The Parker Campsite

Little was said at the breakfast table. Rusty cut his pancakes with his fork and noticed Hurricane Kate cloaking the lower Gulf of Mexico and southern Florida with rain. He poured syrup on his pancakes sighing with relief that Wendy wasn't at the table.

Rusty's mother took her eyes off the television and broke the silence, "Rusty, what are your plans today, honey?"

"I'd like to go to Cal's. We're goin' fishin'. Rusty looked at the television screen. "Oh, no. Small craft warnings. That means we can't go out."

"Then that means Wendy won't be going out, either. It's funny. She didn't tell me she'd be going out with Captain McCoy last night."

Rusty's hand with the orange juice glass froze in mid-air. "Last night?"

"Yes." Diane ran a dish cloth around a plate. "She didn't come in yesterday afternoon so I assumed she was with this Captain McCoy. But when she didn't come home. Oh, I'm concerned, Rusty. I . . . She will be so tired when she gets home."

"If she comes home," Rusty said under his breath.

"What was that?" Diane studied the television for a moment. "It's funny. That storm is supposed to be moving away but I can't see it doing that. And if she's . . ."

"Huh." Rusty swallowed his last bite of pancake. "Wendy didn't return yesterday afternoon and she was gone all night, right?"

Diane nodded.

"Don't you see, Mom?" Rusty poured some orange juice. "You let her get away with everything and now look." Rusty chugged his juice then leaped up. "She's probably all right, Mom. Maybe she's with . . . You know what, I've go to Cal. He might know something. See ya in a little bit." Rusty grabbed his poncho and headed for the door. No kiss, no nothing. He grit his teeth in anger. Thanks, Wendy, you self-centered snob. You'll walk over anyone to get what you want. Look what you're doing to Mom. Do you care? Heck no!

Rusty was almost to the Sapps when his cell phone rang. "Dad!" Rusty told his father what was going on with his mother and Wendy.

"I'm sorry to hear this, Rusty," his father said. "You'd better check every possible place she might be. If she doesn't show up soon, . . . You'd better check with the Ranger, and that Captain. Hang in there for another day, then I'll be back to help. Is there any word on the RV?"

"Still waitin' for the parts. How's the job interview?"

"It looks like I got it. Son, try to keep out of trouble and when Wendy shows up, try to keep away from her, okay?"

"I'll try."

"Good. When I get back I want to go to the National Naval Aviation Museum with you."

"I can't wait."

"Then keep a low profile."

Rusty promised he would. He stuffed his cell phone back in his pocket and continued on to the Sapps.

Rusty found Cal working on his lawn mower. "What's up?

Rusty filled him in.

So she didn't come home?"

Rusty motioned with his hands. "My mom says she hasn't seen her since yesterday afternoon. Sally accused Wendy of holdin' out on her. My guess is she spent the night with Rory and they're at the fort diggin' as we speak."

"That's what I think, too." Cal looked up at Rusty and grinned. "Sally's back? I'll hurry and dust my room, then we can go look for Wendy. Wanna help?"

"Help dust? We have a cleaning lady that comes in and does that."

"Must be nice."

The boys entered the kitchen where Cal pulled a pitcher of lemonade from the refrigerator and poured them both a glass. He then picked up a rag and a can of Pledge.

Not wanting to appear lazy Rusty asked, "Heck. Where's a rag?"

Cal smiled. "You take one side and I'll take the other."

Rusty began dusting an already immaculate room. but paused long enough to examine a model F-4 Wildcat Cal built. The vintage World War II airplane looked real enough to be parked on a aircraft carrier's deck.

"It looks so real, Cal. How'd you do it?"

"Good paint and weatherin'. Finished? Let's go. Oh . . . " Cal paused for a moment. "The autopsy report's in."

"And?"

"Sheriff Raymond told my dad there was blunt trauma to the head and neck."

"That's all?"

"No. Chapman's trachea, you know the tube that goes to the

bronchia?"

"Yeah. It's a good thing I watch *CSI* the way you're talkin'.

"Anyway, that was crushed. So it looks like someone conked Chapman on the head then strangled him."

"Unbelieveable!"

"I guess whoever killed Chapman wanted him good 'n dead."

The boys rode their bikes to the old fort and parked by Bastion D, the burned-out side of Fort Pickens. They avoided the long line of people at the Visitor's Center by climbing over the rubble. Cal scrambled over the rocks like a monkey while Rusty watched his footing and paused for breath every couple of seconds. Once on level ground inside the fort, the boys ran to the south wall. No Wendy.

Cal bent down to look at the dirt. "There's no tracks, Rusty, so she didn't come here."

"If she's not here . . ." Rusty grew solemn. "If she's not here that can only mean one thing."

"We'll search the whole fort." Cal sounded upbeat.

The boys went to the cistern but no Wendy. They retraced their steps to the powder magazine, the mine chambers and officer's quarters but didn't find her. They came back out to the parade grounds and looked around. The sky had grown overcast, a light mist fell and thunder grumbled nearby.

"I wonder what happened to her." Rusty looked down at the grass

"Let's see. Diggin' at sun-up, the sun is just comin' up over . . . there." Cal pointed to the east then slowly lowered his hand and grew solemn. "Let's say, Rusty, that Wendy was with Bucky McCoy last night."

"Yeah?"

"And if you're right about that smaller boat being the *SilverKing*

. . ." Cal shivered and shook his head.

"You're sayin' Bucky McCoy took her smugglin' with him?"

Cal nodded.

An icy sensation washed all other feelings from Rusty. A numbness crept over him. "Cal, if what you're sayin's true, Wendy's in a world of poop. I don't think those guys are gonna let Wendy live."

The two boys stood in silence as the grim realization seeped in, the somber knowledge that Wendy might never get off Santa Rosa Island alive.

Rusty kicked at the grass. Here it was, a girl he hated, a girl who tormented him mercilessly, a girl who had not one kind word to say to him, a girl who shared his blood — now facing certain death. The sensible part of him said take action. "What do we do?" Rusty asked softly.

Cal looked at his friend standing there, looking at the ground. "We'll check the Tower Bastion and counterscarp then get my dad. And maybe we have it all wrong. We'll check out the *SilverKing*."

"Let's go." Rusty took the steps two at a time, ignoring the tourists' dirty looks and got to the Rodman cannon the same time Cal did. He leaned over gasping for breath. "I'm never doin' that again," he panted.

"You really should get more exercise, Rusty," Cal said. "You'd make a good football player."

"I hate football. I hate all sports. Too much work."

"Whatever."

The boys didn't find any sign of Wendy by the moat, the Tower Bastion or the counterscarp. They left Fort Pickens and hurried to Cal's house to get Cal's father.

"Cal," Rusty said on the way to the Sapps. "I was thinkin' of something. Sally didn't seem too upset about her husband's death."

"Different people have different ways of dealin' with something like that. She's probably still in shock."

"Yeah. You're probably right." Rusty got off his bike and pushed the kickstand down. The boys went in for something cold to drink.

Mr. Sapp was not home. Cal's mother said he went to Home Depot for extra plywood to board up the windows — just in case.

Cal kissed his mom then the boys started towards the marina where the water was getting rougher and white caps topped the waves.

They pedaled for a little bit when Rusty stopped. "Cal . . ." He looked at the asphalt. "Wendy kinda blackmailed me."

Cal frowned. "Blackmailed you? How?"

"At school these guys were talkin' about this porn site so I went to it just to see what it was like. And last month *Playboy* had that actress in it, before she became famous, so I had a buddy loan me a copy."

"Yeah? What's wrong with that?"

"Wendy has the run of the house so she came into my bedroom and saw the magazine while I was on the website. Yesterday she woke me up and threatened to tell my mom if I told anyone she was gonna dig for the gold and that she and Rory were gonna run off."

"I don't think Rory Abrams is gonna run off with anybody." Cal blew a lock of hair off his forehead. "Especially an underage girl who can't get a job to support him." A devilish grin crept across Cal's face. "How did those actresses look?"

"Nice," Rusty grinned.

"You still have the copy?"

"Of course."

"We'll look at it later. First we have to find Wendy."

They reached the marina and stopped under the same tree Wendy and Rusty had stopped under earlier in the week.

"Please, God," Cal whispered.

"You really like her, don't you?" Rusty asked.

"Yeah, I guess I do," Cal said.

"I don't know what you see in a positively selfish, weird cousin who's stuck up and thinks she's god's gift to boys."

Cal stopped dead in his tracks and glared at Rusty. "Didn't you say she has a messed up life?"

"Yeah. Her mom and dad are divorced and even when he comes around he always cuts her down, calls her a stupid bimbo and . . . sometimes worse."

"Ow." Cal grimaced.

"Personally, I can't stand the guy even though he's my uncle. And Wendy may be a lot of things but she's none of the things he calls her."

"Listen, Rusty. Underneath all that purple hair, piercings and stuff, that girl pleadin' to be accepted and loved just as she is. That's why she got herself into this mess. She needs a guy to accept her. You don't have to be a shrink to figure it out. It's as plain as the nose on your face."

"I never thought about it, or looked at her that way, Cal."

"Try it." Cal walked toward the *SilverKing*.

"I will," Rusty said. Then he whispered to himself — "If she's still alive."

A SHOCK

The Marina on Santa Rosa Island

At the *SilverKing* a group of fishermen clad in knee-high socks, flowered shirts and weird hats stood on the pier waiting to board. If this was December, Rusty thought, these guys would be the classic snowbirds. There was no sign of Bucky McCoy nor Rory Abrams.

"Have you seen Captain McCoy?" A pipe-smoking fisherman asked.

"No sir, we haven't," Rusty answered.

"We were suppose to go out for a half-day trip but we can't find him." A tall lean man looked at the sky. "Gale warnings are going to go up."

"Gale warnings?" Rusty frowned. "What's goin' on?"

"A hurricane." The tall man scowled. "Don't you watch the news?"

Cal pulled on Rusty's shirt before Rusty could reply. "Come on, we'll check the cabin."

"We'll have to try to sober him up. Do ya know how to make coffee?"

"That doesn't work anymore, Rusty."

"Let's hope for the best."

The door to the cabin was slightly ajar, strange because Wendy was always telling Rusty and Cal how meticulous the Captain was about keeping it closed. Entering the cabin the boys found everything in order. Two wooden chairs were pushed in close to a small matching wooden table. Photographs of Marilyn Monroe — one on the cover of *Life* magazine, and the infamous photograph of the actress in *Playboy,* enshrined in a golden frame, hung on one wall. Coffee cups with Marilyn's face on them hung from a cabinet. Looking in one room, Rusty found a bed neatly made.

Passing by the sink Rusty inadvertently knocked a stack of papers, held down by a conch shell, onto the deck. The shell shattered into hundreds of pink and white shards. I'll clean it up later, Rusty thought. He picked up the papers, noticed a strange one with weird writing on it and also an LSU earring on the deck under the sink. He put the paper with strange writing along with the earring in his pocket then placed the other papers beside the sink and continued looking around.

"Odd." Cal whispered.

"No Wendy," Rusty added. "And where is everybody?" His eyes roved to the photo in the gold frame.

"Stop gawking at the picture, Rusty." Cal pulled his friend around the room. "We've got work to do."

On the wooden table lay an open copy of *Bowditch's Practical Navigation*, Nautical charts of the northern Gulf of Mexico, and two books of Florida fish. Rusty looked at Cal who shook his head.

"Let's check below." Cal headed for the steps that would take them to the head and the engines.

"Just to be on the safe side." Rusty peeked into the head and shower stall and found no one. "Jeez." Rusty stood on a bath mat with a picture of a clipper ship under full sail and bounced about three times.

Cal gave his friend a strange look and laughed. "What are you doing?"

"This feels uneven, not like the rest of the deck. Feel."

Rusty stepped aside and let Cal onto the mat. "Huh."

When Cal stepped off, Rusty pulled the mat away disclosing a hatch with an open lock.

"I'll be darned." Cal stared at the secret door. "Rusty, there's only one reason why Bucky McCoy has a trap door."

Rusty gave Cal a knowing look. "The night before."

"Right."

"Wonder what's down there," Rusty said.

"Let's find out." Cal opened the hatch cover.

A strong smell of bleach and disinfectant wafted up into the head.

"Huh." Cal began the descent into the hold. Rusty followed, careful not to step on Cal's fingers.

The light from the shower room and open door did little to illuminate the hold. Rusty found a rag doll with a soiled white face and stained clothing.

"What's this?" Cal bent over and lifted a pocket-size New Testament off the deck.

"This is weird, Cal, really weird." Rusty tapped Cal's shoulder. "Over there, in the corner. Shhh . . . someone's comin."

From above, the boys heard a familiar voice. "You think he's talking to those three fishermen? The voices faded. Cal and Rusty heard the creaking of the deck and someone singing the Beatles' "Hey Jude."

Rory Abrams entered the cabin and stood ion the deck right over the boys. "Damn him," Rory said. The boys heard a click then a thump. Rory had locked the hatch. In doing so he locked Cal and

Rusty in the hold. The boys heard the sound of footsteps fade — then all was quiet. That is, all was quiet until the boys heard the faint voice on the weather radio telling all boats in the middle and upper Gulf of Mexico to seek safe refuge because Hurricane Kate would be upon them in less that twenty-four hours. Immediately after hearing the announcement, *SilverKing's* engine thundered to life and a safety lantern shed some dim light in the hold.

Rusty and Cal looked at each other. "Where are we going?" Rusty asked.

Cal squinted in the darkness. "Could be anywhere, the Blackwater River, the Mississippi."

"The Mississippi! Cal, we're in deep poop." Rusty's stomach rumbled, then was replaced by a queasiness as the boat crashed through the ever increasing rough waves. "You didn't bring anything to eat, did you?"

"No. Now let me think."

Cal moved over to a corner and slid to the deck. As he placed his left palm on the deck he felt something move beneath it. He picked it up and noticed it was a crucifix on a beaded necklace. "Rusty, take a look."

Rusty took the necklace from Cal and fingered it. "Let's see," Rusty held the necklace up to the dim light, "We have a Bible, a doll and a necklace with a cross on it. What does that tell us?"

The boys could vaguely see each other's face.

"I think I know, Rusty." Cal looked at the hatch. "Bucky McCoy is smuggling illegal aliens into this country."

"And Wendy is in the middle of it! But where?"

"Yeah. And that explains why those old boys were shooting and chasing us the other night. We appeared on their radar and they didn't want any witnesses." Cal slapped his hand on the bulkhead. "Bucky McCoy, a man I've known all my life, turns out to be a criminal."

Rusty didn't say anything. If Cal wants to talk, I'll listen. Cal didn't want to talk. Rusty looked at his friend. Cal just stared at the bulkhead and toyed with the crucifix trying to make sense of what they'd just discovered.

SilverKing slowed and turned. The boat traveled for what the boys thought was a half hour then slowed and came to a stop.

"Now what?" Rusty asked.

"We wait until Rory leaves — then try to get out."

"He's not staying?" Rusty asked.

"I don't think so. I think he brought the boat up here to escape the hurricane."

The boys stayed below until they didn't hear Rory moving around on deck.

"Okay." Cal looked at the hatch. "Rory locked it. So . . ."

Rusty looked around. "I don't see anything to pry the hatch with, and it darn well doesn't look like a cheap lock and latch, either. I don't think we could kick it open?"

Cal patted his pocket. "I've got my Leatherman tool with me. Let's see if we can unscrew it."

"Good idea. But it's so dark. Can you see?"

"Not really, but what choice do we have?"

Cal climbed to the top of the steps, felt around for the screw, and tried to unscrew the latch.

Suddenly, Rusty heard a snap! "You okay, Cal?"

"Yeah, but the screwdriver blade broke."

"Now what?"

"Maybe I can use the knife blade and cut the latch out, but it's gonna take awhile."

The rocking motion of the boat picked up, and Rusty's stomach felt queasy. It was taking a long time for Cal cut around the thick wood. And Rusty was afraid to move around too much. "You want a break? I can try," he offered.

"In a minute."

After a few more minutes, Cal climbed down the stairs. "Okay, I think we're close. You take over. You'll be able to feel where I've been carving away, and you'll feel the screws, too. Just be careful."

After several minutes Cal made his way back up the stairs. "Here, move over." Cal came settled on the same rung. "You push with your hands and I'll kick. On the count of three! Ready?"

Rusty nodded.

"One, two, three!" Cal kicked and Rusty pushed. The hatch splintered into three pieces.

"Let's go!" Rusty scrambled up with Cal on his heels. In the cabin, Rusty paused to take one long last look at the Marilyn photograph in the golden frame.

"C'mon, Rusty, before anyone comes aboard. I'll buy you that photo," Cal whispered urgently. They bounded over the side into waist deep water and waded past clumps of mangroves. Unseen by anyone, they stayed in the canal until they came to a bridge with sandbags leading down to the water. Cars and trucks rumbled over the top of them moving in both directions. The boys scrambled up the sandbags, climbed over an aluminum guard rail and stood on the shoulder of the four-lane highway than ran east and west.

"It must be I-10," Rusty squinted towards the west.

"I don't think we've gone that far." Cal looked in both directions then brightened. "I know where we are. This is the Escambia River.

C'mon." The boys began walking towards the west, cars ignoring them. They had only gone a little ways when Cal shook his head in disbelief. "Doggone Bucky McCoy."

Rusty kicked a pebble into the grass. "And Wendy said Bucky and the boat was missing the other morning. Plus, she said she wasn't allowed to go below deck. Now we know why. Who woulda thought."

"That's why." Cal toyed with the doll. "Although it's clear, now, Wendy woulda saw the hold when *SilverKing* came back, full of poop, puke and whatever."

"Jeez. Bucky McCoy." Rusty stared at a red Porsche convertible flying by. The nice old fisherman who saved a pelican, and gave Wendy a job, was a smuggler. Not of rum or marijuana, but of people. Poor, misfortunate people.

Cal picked up the pace. "When we get back we gotta tell Dad. And we gotta find Wendy — if it's not too late."

THE MISSING THREE

Even though the sky had turned gray, and a light mist fell, sweat ran down the boys necks. Rusty ran his tongue over his parched lips and longed for something cold to drink.

"How far to home?" Rusty asked.

"Not far. Maybe two or three more miles."

"Wonderful," Rusty gasped. "It's like learning your favorite actor is dead"

Cal ran his hand across his forehead. "What is?"

"Bucky McCoy."

"I've known him all my life and never suspected," Cal bemoaned. "Sure, some times we'd come in from the mainland at night and his boat would be gone, but I thought nothing of it."

"I wonder how long he's be doin' it," Rusty said.

Cal, too lost in thought to notice anything said, "I reckon about a year or so. When times started getting rough."

Rusty shook his head. "He told Noah he was about to lose the boat so maybe that's why he began smuggling illegal aliens."

A horn blew and the boys heard a car come to a stop. Rusty turned and saw the red and blue lights in the grill of an unmarked police car. Sheriff Raymond leaned his head out the window and asked if the boys wanted a ride. They accepted the offer and eased into the back seat.

"There's still a better way to do things." Cal pushed the door closed. “Maybe a harder way — but easier on your conscience — and legal.”

“What are you talking about?” The sheriff asked.

The boys informed the lawman about Bucky McCoy’s smuggling operation and the fact they were shot at.

“I’ll check into it after the hurricane.” The sheriff looked in the rearview mirror. “Boys, this one’s gonna be a doozey.”

Rusty fidgeted, then reached into his pocket for the strange paper and the LSU earring. He unfolded the paper and nudged Cal, handing him the paper and the earring.

Words cut from magazines and glued to the paper read: “0100. Three miles off Cooper Battery.”

“It’s three-thirty now,” Cal said. “It’s been over thirteen hours. And what’s with the earring?”

“Sally Chapman is a LSU fan and wears them. What’s Cooper Battery?”

“An old World War Two gun on a nature trail.” Cal looked at the note one more time. “And what was Sally Chapman doing aboard the *SilverKing*?”

“It’s that Geron . . . Cal!”

“Huh?”

“I know how it played out.”

“You’re kiddin’, right?”

“I wish I was. Look, Wendy wasn’t at the fort. She wasn’t on the boat. She probably went back to Bucky McCoy to get Rory. Then seein’ the *SilverKing* come in, she goes aboard. Wendy said she was going diggin’. That would save Bucky a lotta work. Plus, I know my cousin, Cal. When someone tells her not to do something, she’s gonna do it anyway — just for spite.”

Rusty looked out the window. "Bucky told her to not go below, and guess what? Wendy went below and got caught. And somehow Sally Chapman is involved."

Cal thought for a minute then said, "I hope you're wrong, Rusty but I get the feelin' you're not. And Rory."

Rusty gave the paper one more glance then said, "Speaking of which, where is he?"

"Who?"

"Rory."

Cal glanced at Rusty and then at the sheriff. "Somebody probably picked him up. I reckon he's with Bucky now."

"Say he is, Cal. Why didn't he leave a note saying the *SilverKing* was closed for the morning? It doesn't take that long to scribble a note. That's just bad business." Rusty lowered his voice. "The question is, where are they now?"

"Who knows?" Cal shrugged. "This gets stranger by the minute."

"Boys," Sheriff Raymond cracked his gum. "I can't tell you what to do, but I suggest, if you're gonna do anything, make it fast 'cause that hurricane is travelin' mighty quick and should be here within twenty-four hours. You leave this missing girl and Bucky McCoy to us. You've already told me those ol' boys shot at you and that should tell you something right there."

The boys said they would and asked the lawman to drop them off at the marina so they could get their bikes. The sheriff's car came to a halt, and the officer got out and opened the passenger's door for the Cal and Rusty. They thanked him quickly and jumped out. Already the sky had turned black and the mist had become a light rain.

National Hurricane Center — FIU

The commotion of bustling people talking on telephones and clacking away on computers, ricocheted off the walls.

"We know Kate didn't read the computer forecast." Hurricane Specialist Sidney Greenspan stood at the map on the wall with Angie Soto.

Angie frowned. "This isn't the time for jokes, Sid."

Larry Rhodes burst into the room. "That high pressure area that just developed is pushing Kate straight up the Gulf. I've put a hurricane warning out for the Panhandle from Tallahassee to Biloxi. Sid, did you contact the Navy and Eglin Air Force Base?"

Greenspan said he did.

"Alright, Ang. What do you think?"

"She's directly across from Naples, now. I think, and the computers will back me on this, at the speed she's moving, Kate will make landfall between eight this evening and midnight around Pensacola. Santa Rosa Island will take a direct hit."

"Thanks. Okay, we've got work to do. I'll notify the governor. The boss will notify the White House." Rhodes was still talking as he exited through the glass partitions.

Santa Rosa Island — At the Same Time

Drenched with rain, the boys were relieved to get to Cal's home.

Mr. Sapp was preparing for the coming storm by checking the generator in the garage. If they needed it after the storm, he could drag it outside and crank it up.

"Your mother has gone to the store for bread, extra canned goods and water." Mr. Sapp motioned towards the plywood. "If you boys help me with boarding the windows, I'll go down and see what we can do about the R.V."

The boys held a large sheet of plywood while Mr. Sapp screwed the top left corner into place, covering a window. While doing so the boys told him of their discovery of Bucky McCoy's smuggling operation.

"Doesn't surprise me none." Mr. Sapp removed a screw from his pocket. "The man's done everything outside the law you can think of — plus some stuff you couldn't think of." Cal's father screwed the bottom right side of plywood into place. "He should have been in jail a long time ago but he always comes out smellin' like a rose."

A half-hour later, the Sapp's home was boarded up, and shortly after, Mrs. Sapp came in reporting how she had to stand in line and how the supplies on the shelves were quickly vanishing.

Rusty pedaled towards the RV. The Sapps assured him they'd follow shortly. He looked at the water and saw how choppy it had become. The once blue gulf was now boiling and black, whitecaps decorating the top of the waves like froth on a mug of root beer. The sun hid behind thick clouds, the breeze picked up and the mist turned into a heavier rain. The sky is the blackest I've ever seen, Rusty thought, like my mood if anything happens to Wendy.

Like Cal said, she's pleadin' to be accepted and loved as she is. She needs a male to accept her as she is. The words echoed in Rusty's head. That explains a lot. Uncle Dave certainly hasn't been a shining light in Wendy's life. I'll try to understand her more if . . . she's alive.

Rusty walked into the RV and asked his mother if she'd heard anything from Wendy.

"No and I'm getting worried, Rusty." Diane looked out through the window at the darkened sky. "People are leaving the island in hoards." He had never seen his mother look so concerned. "Rusty, do you know anything about your cousin?"

You wouldn't believe me if I told you, he thought. Out loud he said, "I'll wait 'till the Sapps get here. I'm goin' outside to start pickin' things up."

Rusty began folding the chairs, securing them in the RV. The wind was so powerful he had a hard time holding on to them. The rain peppered down. He folded the last chair just as the Sapps drove up.

"Any word?" Cal asked.

"No." Rusty swallowed hard. "Now we have to do the inevitable. But Cal." Rusty grabbed his friend's arm.

"Yeah?"

"Do you think Bucky McCoy would sell Wendy?"

"I don't know, Rusty. I'd like to think not." Cal wiped the rain from his forehead. "I believe he's just into hauling them aliens but who really knows a person?"

"And I'm still confused about that earring." Rusty's heart sank. "I guess it's time."

Rusty and Cal watched a stream of cars leaving the park for the safety of the mainland and western Georgia as they finished tying things down. They halted what they were doing as they saw Rory Abrams leaving the campground.

National Hurricane Center — FIU

"She's a Category Five hurricane now. Look at the eye and the feeder bands." Angie Soto looked at the satellite images of Kate.

Larry Rhodes took a sip from his ever-present cup of coffee and saw the bright yellow and red blobs rapidly turn in a counter-clock-wise movement up the Gulf. "It's a textbook hurricane. What does the MEOW say?"

The MEOW (Maximum Envelope of Water) computer forecast predicted water fifteen feet above normal to come ashore. Since water weighs sixty-four pounds per cubic foot, Pensacola was in for a beating. This was the storm surge, the water pushed towards land by a hurricane. As water reaches the shallow coast, it slows, piles up then comes ashore rapidly. It does not come ashore as a tidal wave like Hollywood likes to show in it's movies.

"How's the evacuation going?" Rhodes asked.

"Better than expected. The governor has issued a mandatory evacuation notice. There's still a few holdouts. You know, the elderly who refuse to leave their homes, plus the idiots who plan to throw a hurricane party."

"I just hope they live to throw another one."

A DEADLY DATE

The Parker Campsite, Santa Rosa Island

"Why would anyone want to kidnap Wendy?" Diane Parker wrung her hands as she tried to decide what or what not to put in a suitcase. "Especially with a hurricane coming. And a murder! What are we coming to?"

"I know why," Rusty piped up.

"Why, Rusty?" His mother asked skeptically.

"It's that Geronimo's gold thing, Miz Parker," Cal said. "Plus, we have evidence that Bucky was involved in illegal alien smuggling."

"What? You mean someone would actually kill over a myth?"

"I tried to tell you Mom," Rusty threw his hands up. "But you didn't believe me."

"'Pears so," Cal's father said. "Have a seat Miz Parker. There's a very good possibility that Bucky kidnapped Wendy."

"Oh my God." Diane collapsed into the back of the chair. "This is too much."

Don Sapp explained. "Every time that old fishin' guide gets drunk he tells people he knows where Geronimo's gold is. But in reality it's nonexistent. Now, from what the boys tell me he's into smugglin' illegal aliens into this country."

"So Warren Chapman tried to get Wendy to find out where the gold is . . . was . . . whatever. And Rusty, you say you heard Rory and Noah McCoy talking about the gold and killing you and Wendy?" Diane sat down. "That is so twisted it's pathetic. Now you say this Bucky McCoy is into human trafficking?"

"It's what we found on the boat, Mom." Rusty pointed. "Uh-oh, look at that."

Diane had the television tuned to the local news. The eye of Kate was even with Ft. Myers but the feeder bands were already coming ashore on Santa Rosa Island. The wind had picked up and the light mist that fell earlier turned into a hard rain.

Cal's mother, Becky, placed a box of Dunkin Donuts and styrofoam cups of coffee on the table. "Noah and I went all through school together. After he graduated he joined the Marines and was in Desert Storm." Mrs. Sapp took a sip of coffee. "He came back a changed man, got some job with the government and was gone a lot. His wife got tired of him being gone all the time and found a boyfriend. Noah went through a bitter divorce. We all felt sorry for him because he was a good man. I don't think he's capable of anything illegal."

"I agree with with my wife," Mr. Sapp said. "Now, imagine in your mind Central and South America. Honduras, Nicaragua, Costa Rica, even Colombia, South America are on the Caribbean Sea and Gulf of Mexico side. These are poor countries. People are promised a better life here in the U.S. They literally sell their souls to come here. Often, the aliens are jammed onto a freighter, the freighter stops just outside the twelve mile limit, Bucky McCoy goes out at night, gets the misfortunate people and brings them ashore. No customs, no nothing — except good money. Just like smugglin' drugs."

"Wow!" Rusty said.

"Yes. They came here for a better life but look what they'll wind up with." Mrs. Sapp refilled any empty coffee cups. "Low paying jobs, the jobs no one else wants, prostitution maybe. Living with five other families in a small house. It's not a pleasant picture."

"Exactly." Cal's father looked at his watch. "Now, Miz Parker, finish packin' and get ready to evacuate. It's seven o'clock. The main part is supposed to hit between eight and midnight and the governor has issued a mandatory evacuation notice. You haven't much time. The Sheriff is conductin' a search for your niece."

Diane pushed the suitcase across the bed. "Mr. Sapp, I will not leave this island without my niece. I owe her that much."

"What do you owe me, Mom?"

Diane waved him off. "Rusty, I don't have time for that nonsense right now. And what about this RV, Mr. Sapp?"

Cal's father heaved a heavy sigh and reached for his poncho. "Ah don't mean to sound smart-alecky, ma'm, but I assume you have insurance on it?"

Diane gave Cal's father a dirty look. "Yes, yes we do."

"Then ah recommend you leave it and git to higher ground. We'll find your Wendy."

Diane folded her arms. "No."

Rusty hung his head and looked at the floor. She loves Wendy more than me. She's risking both our lives for Wendy. Would she risk her and Wendy's life for me? Nah, probably not. Rusty picked up the box, picked out a jelly donut then handed the box to Cal. "Want one, Cal?"

"No thanks." Cal turned his attention to the television.

Crack! Crash! Everyone jumped as a large branch fell close to the RV.

"I don't mean to upset you, but we don't have time to argue,

Mrs. Parker. My suggestion is to leave. The Governor and Sheriff don't take kindly to people disobeyin' an evacuation notice."

"They can stay at the house, Donnie," Becky Sapp told her husband.

"Ah don't even like you bein' there, Rebecca. So close to the water."

"We've been through it before, Don."

"But not like this one." Don Sapp looked at his watch. "It's seven-thirty. We're wastin' time. Look how bad it's getting. Do as you please. Rebecca, you have my cell phone. All the windows are boarded up and the generator is fueled up. Keep me posted." He pecked her cheek and walked out into the rain.

"Get packed and come to the house before it really gets bad." Cal's mother washed the empty cups and put them back in the RV's cabinet.

"Thank you, Becky, we will." Diane managed a grateful smile. "Rusty get ready."

In less than ten minutes Rusty stuffed his poncho pockets full of Twinkies, his suitcase full of graphic novels, and he and his mother were in the backseat of the Sapp's Chevy Blazer headed to the their modest home, that had stood through a hundred hurricanes.

The Sapp Home

"It's strange there's no word from the kidnappers," Diane paced the Sapp's living room, then paused to stare out the window at the trees bending almost horizontally and the waves hitting the concrete seawall and blasting up into the air.

"Just the note on Mr. McCoy's boat." Rusty said.

"They have what they want, Miz Parker," Cal said. "Wendy."

"Sit down, Diane, until we figure this thing out." Cal's mother turned the television on then poured two cups of coffee. A news lady stood with the churning Gulf behind her; one hand holding the poncho on her head, the other hand holding the microphone, rain splattering the camera lens. The woman had to lean into the wind and was barely heard.

Diane did not sit down. She began to pace the living room. "I can't eat and I can't sit here and do nothing. I'll go out of my mind."

Rusty rubbed his eyes and looked at the Weather Channel. "The hurricane is closing in," he said.

Thunk! A piece of debris hit the side of the house.

Becky Sapp poured herself a cup of coffee then refilled Diane's. "I know how you feel." She grabbed the keys to the Blazer. "Cal, get your poncho and come with us. Rusty, stay here in case something happens. We'll be right back." Cal's mother put her left arm through her rain slicker. "C'mon, Diane, we're going to drive by the RV and drive down to Pensacola Beach then turn around and head for Ft. Pickens. We'll be back soon."

"Why can't I come?" Rusty eyed a box of cookies on top of the refrigerator.

"Someone needs to stay here in case Wendy shows up," Diane explained. "Here's my cell phone. I'm ready."

"But your heart, Mrs. Sapp." Rusty protested.

"My heart is fine, Rusty." Rebecca Sapp ran her left hand through Rusty's hair. "It's kind of you to think of me, but I know my limitations." She looked at Cal and Diane. "let's go." The women and boy fastened their rain gear then ran out to the Blazer.

Deadly Danger

National Hurricane Center — FIU

BULLETIN

HURRICANE KATE ADVISORY NUMBER 10

NATIONAL WEATHER SERVICE MIAMI FL

...DANGEROUS HURRICANE KATE CLOSING IN ON FLORIDA PANHANDLE...

...A HURRICANE WARNING IS IN EFFECT FROM PERRY FLORIDA TO BILOXI, MISSISSIPPI. A HURRICANE WARNING MEANS HURRICANE CONDITIONS IN THE WARNED AREA ARE EXPECTED WITHIN 24 HOURS. PREPARATIONS TO PROTECT LIFE AND PROPERTY SHOULD BE RUSHED TO COMPLETION.

...MAXIMUM SUSTAINED WINDS ARE NEAR 150 MPH WITH HIGHER GUSTS. KATE IS A STRONG CATEGORY 5 ON THE SAFFIR/SIMPSON SCALE AND COULD GET STRONGER BEFORE LANDFALL.

HURRICANE FORCE WINDS EXTEND OUTWARD UP TO ONE HUNDRED TEN MILES FROM THE CENTER...

"We've done all we can," Angie said, reading the latest advisory. She had seen her share of hurricane devastation, from her native Cuba to the Atlantic and Caribbean, as a meteorologist in the Navy. "God help the Panhandle," she prayed, watching the first feeder bands hit Santa Rosa Island as Kate kept her deadly date with Escambia County.

Pensacola, Perry and the Florida Panhandle

Rusty listened as the newscaster reported that not a piece of plywood or a generator could be found at Lowe's or Home Depot. He continued: saying that bread, water and canned food was also in short supply.

Rusty paced the Sapp's living room. I gotta do something. He absently picked up book three of *A Series of Unfortunate Events*, thumbed through it, not looking at it, then laid it down. But what?

Bang! He jumped as an empty wind-blown garbage can hit the side of the house.

"What to do, what to do, what to do." Rusty said outloud as he opened a Twinkie. "I'm suppose to stay here, but . . ."

Rusty spun around and stuffed the remaining half of the Twinkie in his mouth. "There's a hurricane outside but it's our only chance."

Rusty put his left arm through his poncho. "Let's see what we've got. They have to be at Ft. Pickens. It appears Bucky can't, or doesn't, drive and three people plus a big bird can't fit in Rory's or the Chapman's pick-up. And I don't think Noah McCoy's friends would want a pelican for any length of time in their new Dodge Charger. Plus, with this hurricane and mandatory evacuation, no motel is gonna offer them a room. So they have to be at the fort." Rusty zipped his poncho. "Why didn't we see them? Because they probably hid until they heard us go by, then moved. I've done enough talkin'. Now it's time for action."

Rusty glanced at the television and saw waves crashing over the empty bridge. The newscaster was saying the bridge was closed and if you weren't off Santa Rosa Island — it was too late. Rusty pulled the hood of his parka over his head and leaned his body against the wind-battered door.

He bent into the wind, navigating fallen branches, flying debris and, worst of all, power lines that began to snap and arc. Why am I doing this? Rusty wondered as the rain pelted his face and the wind drove him sideways. Ft. Pickens is only a short distance, but I doubt if I'll ever make it. At least I'll die a hero . . . or an attempted one.

On the Road to Pensacola Beach

"We'll find her." Becky Sapp leaned her head out the Blazer's window. If only I believed that myself, she thought. The torrential downpour made it impossible to see. Wind rocked the sturdy Blazer unmercifully as Diane grasped the seat with both hands while Becky clutched the steering wheel in a death-like grip.

"Maybe we should go back, Becky." Diane looked at the angry wind bend trees almost to the ground. "This wasn't such a good idea after all. Besides, I don't like leaving Rusty alone."

"He'll be fine. We'll be back before you know it." Becky pulled her head back in, wiped her face with a towel then swerved to miss a large puddle.

She slowed the Blazer, stuck her head out the window again, then stopped. She pulled her head back in and wiped the rain off her face. "Wow! Look."

Kate had uprooted and blown a very large tree across the road.

"There's no place to turn around, is there?" Diane looked out the rain splattered windows in all directions.

"No, but Mom." Cal leaned over the front seat. "Dad has a chain in the back. We can wrap the chain around the trunk and maybe pull the tree off the road."

"Good idea, son." Becky smiled. "Will you help us, please?"

"Sure."

Up ahead the beam of headlights sparkled in the rain.

"Who could be out in weather like this?" Diane asked.

"Probably the sheriff or EMS. Ready?" Becky put the Blazer in park and all three leaped out into the storm.

Becky opened the back and after a few minutes of searching, Cal produced a thick, heavy chain.

"You take one end and wrap it around the tree." Cal handed one end to his mother, shouting to be heard above the wind and rain. "I'll take the other end and put it on a hook under the bumper."

Both women gasped as the tempestuous wind took their breath away and. Despite their ponchos, the rain stung their cheeks and foreheads. The job took longer than normal due to the darkness, the ferocious wind and the blinding rain.

"Now." Becky closed the Blazer door. "You have it good and secure?"

Cal nodded.

"Good. Here." Becky handed Diane and Cal a towel to dry themselves. "Let's go."

The rear tires spun on the slick road before gaining traction. Slowly the Blazer pulled the tree to the side.

"Uh-oh. Look." Cal pointed to a lone person with a fading flashlight beam silhouetted in the headlights. The figure fought the storm as it walked towards them in. "You have to be nuts walking in weather like this. Let's undo the chain and see who it is." Becky jammed the Blazer into park. "Whoever it is might be needs help."

The flashlight the figure held flickered out.

After putting the chain back in the Blazer the women noticed the person was only yards in front of them. Becky put the Blazer in gear and moved towards the figure. Once alongside, she rolled down the window, shielding her face. "You need help."

"Could you drive me to Ft. Pickens," a familiar voice said.

Diane stopped drying her face and looked in shock at the pale, wet, hollowed-eyed face. “Rory! Are you alright?”

Just then a power pole snapped sending a shower of sparks over the street.

“Get in. Get in!”

“Water’s over the road down there, but I’ll be fine as soon as I reach the Fort.”

“Have you seen Wendy?” Diane asked. “Is she . . . Ft. Pickens?”

“You can stay at our house, Rory,” Becky offered. “Until the storms over.”

“It’s just I have some unfinished business at the Fort.” Rory reached into his raincoat and brought out a handkerchief and wiped his face. When he stuffed it back in he produced something else. “I know you’ll take me.”

The electrical sparks shined on something silver in Rory Abrams’ hand. The two women and boy looked at the object and froze when they saw a .357 Ruger pointed at Cal’s chest.

BIG TROUBLE ON A LITTLE ISLAND

On the Road to Ft. Pickens

I'll go in and surprise them, Rusty said to himself and reached for a tree branch, a railing — anything to support him against the wind. He walked two steps forward and was blown back four. Behind him a pair of headlights bounced off the rain.

A Porta-Potty bounced once, twice across the road then ended up in a deep puddle. This rain stings worse than fire-ant bites, Rusty thought. And sound is unbearable blowing in my ears. It almost borders on pain. I should never have come out in this.

If they're there, we should all wait until the eye comes then get Cal's dad. Whoa! Rusty ducked as a folding beach chair barely missed him. My life was nice and peaceful until I came on this vacation. Now it's never gonna be the same. Rusty chuckled in spite of the danger. Think of what I'll tell my grandkids if I ever get married. Right, fat chance.

The headlights grew brighter, shining like diamonds in the rain, eerily lighting the road. What is a car doin' out in weather like this? Rusty shielded his eyes, peered at the car then quickened his pace. The headlights now fully illuminated him. Thank goodness, there's the fort!

Snap! Crack! Crackle! Crash! Rusty jumped to the left as a telephone pole broke in half and slammed across the road. The falling pole narrowly missed Rusty, the impact spraying him with mud, leaves and a faceful of water. Visibly shaken, he looked around. The arcing electric wires showed savage waves, waves that would have been great to surf, hurdled towards shore. Constantly battling the wind and rain, pausing briefly and vainly to wipe his face, Rusty stared at the wreckage before moving on.

What happened to those headlights? Rusty thought as he trudged on. The wind, rain, small bits of debris and branches battered him. He slogged towards Ft. Pickens. Whoa! A gust of wind pushed him backwards — almost knocking him over. He felt water coming up to his knees. Storm surge. I remember that from school. The water will be coming in fast. I've got to get to Ft. Pickens or else I'll drown. Rusty kept moving an inch at a time, often being blown backwards and sidestepping utility poles that broke like a toothpicks. Then, after an eternity and through the deluge, Rusty stood at the entrance of the majestic fort. The visitor's center and sally port gates were locked. Rusty shivered. If I get any colder I'll be an ice cube.

Through the rain Rusty saw the burned out section of Bastion D. He slogged over to the area and began to climb the rubble. He climbed only a few inches when he slipped, banging his head, arms and legs against the bricks. In addition to being cold, pain ripped through his body making this a lesson in pure agony. Ow, my head. He ran his fingers over his head and felt two growing lumps — one at the base of his skull and one at the top. He then looked down at the torn knee in his jeans, if there was any blood the rain had washed it away.

There was no time for further examination. The water was rising fast. Slowly, slower than he cared to go, Rusty began to climb. Hurry. No. Ugh! I'm doing fine. I'll reach for this brick. Heave! That brick. This brick . . . oh no! Once again Rusty slipped on the wet bricks.

This time he caught himself. I'm going to lay off the Twinkies, start running and lifting weights . . . if I survive this. Whew! There's the top. Oh no! A gust of wind almost knocked him back down. Rusty felt himself slipping, his fingers sliding off the rain-soaked bricks. No, I'm not going through that again. He clamped down tighter on the bricks and lifted himself up.

Finally. Thank goodness, Rusty thought as he reached the top and swayed back and forth in the wind. He dropped to the ground. How do I climb down without slipping? He only managed a few inches before he slipped and slid until he hit the ground — the pain in his aching head, knees and back telling him they didn't appreciate what he'd just done, but he could move, so he wasn't badly hurt. Now what? Rusty scanned the area and tried to hear something above the hurricane. I know they're here — but where? And what do I do? Wait until Kate blows over and get Mr. Sapp? That may be too late. I've got to get started and hopefully I'll think of something.

To his left stood the visitor's center, across from that the officer's quarters. He entered the room and moved to the left. No one was there. He moved down to the mine battery room. That compartment was vacant, too.

Outside, Kate took her toll. The familiar yacht, *Ramblin' Rose* broke free of her moorings and drifted aimlessly toward the Florida/Alabama border. *Fun Seeker*, *Sloe Jim*, and *Miss Behavin'* followed. Next went the docks, piers and houses — structures that had withstood one hundred and twenty mile an hour winds disintegrated beneath the massive wind and storm surge. Homes built right along the Gulf crumbled like a stack of dominoes. Vehicles and roads were swept out to sea. Mobile home parks looked like huge metal recycling yards. Trailers that were not ripped apart were flipped upside down. Stoplights crashed onto streets. Windows, three stories up, shattered. Five people were already known dead while scores were missing or injured. What was once a proud island, Santa Rosa was nothing but a long sandbar. And Kate's center was still five miles out. Yet, while chaos loomed all around, Ft. Pickens stood fast.

Rusty cautiously stuck his head into the powder magazine. He couldn't see or hear anyone. The only area left to check out were the mine chambers.

Already fatigued by his long ordeal, Rusty took a deep breath, bent over, and began to waddle toward the two forks. Electricity being knocked out due to Kate, he had to keep one hand on the damp wall as he plodded along the dark corridor. The forks can't be far away, he thought. This struggle is getting old. Then he heard voices and saw light flicker off a wall to his left. Rusty stopped and listened.

"You have twenty seconds to tell us what you did with the gold." A familiar male voice growled

"I tell you, I don't have the gold. I never found it," Wendy replied. "Maybe there is no gold."

"There's gold, Wendy. Tell me or else."

"Or else what?" Wendy answered.

"I know some people who would really appreciate some charming young ladies like y'all." Bucky McCoy snickered.

"You can't hurt my mom!" he heard Cal Sapp yell.

Rusty leaned against the wall and took a deep breath. Wendy, Mrs. Sapp and Cal. My gosh! Mrs. Sapp and her heart! If anything happens to her . . . Is there anyone else?

"Please don't hurt my niece. She's done nothing to you." Rusty recognized his mother's voice.

"Except use me and get me drunk for her own purposes."

Mom! Rusty fought to control the tremors that flowed over him.

"It's not like you didn't want to get drunk, Bucky." Noah McCoy's laughter reverberated through the chamber.

"Yer not funny, Noah."

"I wish that damn Sally hadn't gotten away," Rory mused. "She could cause problems."

"Enough. Tie the women up."

"You're not going to hurt Wendy, you jerk!" Cal shouted.

Despite the gravity of the situation, Rusty perked up a little. If only I can get him out of there.

"Noah, bring the girl up here," McCoy ordered.

"No! Please!" Diane cried.

"Let go of her," Cal demanded.

"Aunt Diane, we've tried everything," Wendy said weakly. "Nothing's going to work. If only Rusty woulda got off his big fat butt and . . ."

"You're about to die and still raggin' on Rusty?" Cal asked incredulously. "For your information, Wendy, Rusty is probably out looking for you right now, and the water is coming in off the Gulf fast. As far as I know he could be washed out to sea by this time."

"Oh my god! He was suppose to stay home."

"He ain't like that, Miz Parker."

Diane sobbed. "My son. My precious, precious son."

"Enough of this sentimentality," McCoy snapped. "Where's the gold, Wendy?"

"Where you said it was," Wendy murmured.

"That ain't good enough. You have it!"

"Bucky, we can't do anything until this hurricane is done with."

Noah McCoy's voice echoed through the chamber. "Granted, we could use the money but the Feds are going to be thick as fleas on the island and this part of the Panhandle. Why don't we just take them out to that island we went to as kids and leave them there?"

"Let me think about it."

"If you know what's good for you, young lady you'll let go of my arm," McCoy said sharply.

"Excuse me." Rory piped up. "That's no way to treat a lady."

"What do ye mean, Rory?" McCoy asked.

"I mean Wendy's going to get the gold and she and I are out of here."

"Are yer crazy?" Bucky asked. "I thought it was gonna be me, you and Noah. Put that gun down."

"Ha! Fat chance. You put the gun down and get over there with the rest of them."

"Rory! You are serious about me!" Wendy stated.

"Dead serious, sweetheart. Just a few more hours."

"Rory, you'll be breaking every law in the books," Diane said. "Wendy is just a child."

"And a lovely child at that."

"Stop waving that gun, Rory," Noah demanded.

"Wendy, if Rory double-crossed Sally and killed Warren he'll do the same to you," Cal warned.

"You're just jealous, Cal," Wendy said.

"By tonight baby, we'll be in New Orleans partying the night away."

"I can't wait," Wendy cried.

Rusty wrung both hands in desperation. Time is running out. Now what? Surely Mr. Sapp knows his wife and son are missing. Do

I go to the main corridor and wait for him? No, it'll be all over by that time. Think! Rusty put his hand in the right pocket of his poncho. He felt something squishy in a plastic wrapper. He pulled it out and felt what once was a Twinkie was now a mass of crumbs. He pulled out the rest and discovered they were in the same condition.

Nuts! Rusty put his hand in the left pocket and felt another bag. Is there some other food in there that I forgot about? Rusty pulled the bag out and felt something round. It was the fireworks he purchased when he, Cal and Wendy went to the fireworks stand.

Yes, Rusty smiled. That should work . . . hopefully.

"Rory! What are you doing? Get that gun away from my head," Wendy cried.

"You're right. You're much more valuable to me alive than dead."

"What?" Wendy cried. "You said it was gonna be you and me in New Orleans."

"I changed my mind. All my life I had to work or steal for what I needed. Now, once you give me the gold I'll live like a king in all his splendor. I'll have any woman I want."

A deathly catacomb-like silence drifted over the mine chamber. The only sounds were wind pummeling the island, waves battering the shore and Wendy weeping uncontrollably. Each occupant was waiting for the next move.

Quickly, Rusty reached in the bag and pulled out a cherry bomb. He reached in his pocket, frowned and patted both pockets of the poncho. What good are fireworks without matches? Darn it! He leaned his head against the wall. How could I have been so stupid? Darn, darn, darn. I'm going to get help. I may not save Wendy but I'll save everyone else.

Glumly, Rusty bent over and began the arduous crabwalk to the corridor. I'll never get to see Wendy the way Cal saw her. I'll never get to try to understand her. Darn it all! Wendy' right, I am a retard. Tears of frustration slid down Rusty's face. I failed. I friggin' failed.

Rusty heard the voices grow faint as he crawled down the passageway.

"When the eye comes I'm outta here," Rory said.

"An' jist where do ye think yer' gonna go?" Bucky asked. "There's the second half of the storm to come."

"I thought you loved me," Wendy sobbed.

"I've done my time in prison. Why would I want to go back?"

"You know, Rory. I kinda looked up to you," Cal piped in.

"Really?"

"Yeah. Your lifestyle, man. Free and easy. Work when you want. Party when you want. Any woman you want. Who wouldn't wanna live like that?"

Rusty stopped. I thought I heard something. He continued on. Guess not.

"Cal, you could have picked a better role model," Becky said.

"Nah, Mom. Rory's my hero."

Above all the voices, the wind, the rain, Wendy's crying was the loudest.

"For god's sake, you didn't have to break her heart!" Diane yelled.

"Well, Noah. This is what it all comes down to, ain't it?" Bucky McCoy said.

"I guess. And all this time, Bucky," Noah said, "we could have been rich. Now some crazy fool is going to get that gold."

"Fool? You callin' me a crazy fool?" Rory yelled. "Let me tell you something, Mr. Perfect. I watched you in track. I watched you win the State Title and all the girls flock around you. I watched you go off to Saudi Arabia and come back a hero. I laughed my guts out when Tricia dumped you. Who did she run to? Me!" Rory laughed.

"She always did have bad taste except for me — which didn't last," Noah said.

"Why don't I kill all of you?" Rory cackled.

"No!"

Rusty heard the slide of the pistol as Rory put the gun to some-one's head.

"Rory, Rory, Rory," Noah sighed. "You always were a little bit slow. How, how do you plan to get off this island? Put the gun down and let me handle it."

"No. Noah, I never did like you and if you don't back off you and Wendy'll be the first to go."

THE EYE OF THE STORM

Ft. Pickens

The cries of protest and angry shouts, emitting from the mine chamber, rumbled down the corridor — added to Rusty's frustration. He jumped as Rory fired the handgun to quiet the hostages.

"Shut up or you'll die," he warned.

Even Kate seemed to obey the man. The rain ceased and wind calmed. The eye of the storm had arrived over Ft. Pickens.

"The eye's here. Get up, Wendy."

"No! Don't pull my hair. I'll go with you."

Thunk! Plop! Crash!

"My knee!" Rory cried. "You little . . . where's my gun?"

"Hey man. Sorry," Cal said softly. "I didn't know you . . ."

Cal, you're a genius. Uh-oh. Rusty heard a mad scramble. A flashlight flickered on and Bucky McCoy said, "now before I was rudely interrupted. Rory, you sniveling little cockroach, get over with the rest of them."

"C'mon, Bucky, don't kill me," Rory pleaded.

"I would but you ain't worth the bullet. Come here, Wendy."

Darn. We're back where we started. What a geek! Why would I have fireworks and no matches? I should have taken them out of my poncho when I got home that day. But I'm not going to give up. I may be retarded, but Mom says I'm stubborn. This is where it's going to pay off.

There it was again. He heard shuffling and saw . . . A red LED light. Rusty stopped and listened. Who is it?

"Is that you, Rusty?" A female voice whispered.

"Ms. Chapman? How did you get here?" Rusty waddled up to her.

"It's a long story. I never should have gone up against Bucky and Rory by myself. I should have waited for Noah."

Rusty wiped his forehead. "I don't understand."

Sally put her hand on his shoulder. "Rusty, Noah and I are Treasury agents. We've been after Warren for a long, long time. Now, fill me in on what's going on in there."

"Do you have a lighter?"

"I might. Why?"

Rusty told her about the fireworks and his plan to use them.

"It's as good a plan as I can come up with. Especially since we're dealing with a crazy man. Let's see." The Treasury agent tapped her shorts pocket and pulled out a Zippo. She guided him back to the chamber. "Let's do it."

With their backs to the wall, Rusty pulled out a cherry bomb. "Do you want to?" he asked Sally.

"Nah. You can start the festivities. I'll do the next one."

Rusty put his thumb on the lighter's wheel and flipped down. When a flame spouted, Rusty lit the cherry bomb and lobbed it into the mine chamber. The firecracker fell short and the spark went out — but not before causing a distraction.

"Hear that?" Bucky asked.

"I didn't hear nothing but these damn sniffling women," Noah replied.

"Check it out."

"You check it out. It's dark out there."

"I'll go." Cal spoke up. "I'm not afraid."

"No, I'll go." Mrs. Sapps volunteered.

"Let the kid check," Bucky ordered. "That'll keep any funny stuff from happenin'."

Good, thought Rusty. He could hear Cal's footsteps grow louder and louder. Then, when Cal was right next to him, Rusty grabbed Cal and covered his mouth, pulling him into the deep shadows.

"Cal, I thought you were a goner," Rusty whispered.

"I thought so, too — until now. That Bucky and Rory are insane."

"Are you okay?"

His eyes began to adjust to the darkness and he could make out another figure. "Whose that?"

"Ms. Chapman."

Rusty gave Cal a light jab in the ribs. "They didn't hit our moms, did they?"

"No, but Bucky and Rory aim to kill somebody if they don't walk away from here with the gold. Wait a minute." Cal backed even closer to the wall. "Here we are, just us three. How do you plan to save everybody?"

"Ms Chapman and Noah are Treasury agents. If we can get Noah out here we may have a chance. Remember those firecrackers we bought the other day?" Rusty explained his plan.

"Jensen," Sally said, "Sally Jensen. Not Sally Chapman.

"They didn't get wet?" Cal asked.

"That first one lit."

"Cool. Remind me to use that brand of plastic bags from now on. Listen!"

"That kid's been gone long enough," McCoy said, his voice trailing down the hall. "Go see what's keeping him."

"He probably got lost," Noah replied.

"Go!"

The boys heard shuffling as Noah exited the mine chamber. After a few minutes, they heard something. "Pssst! Noah! Over here."

"What the . . ." Noah crawled over to the three.

"Ms. Chapman, ah . . . Jensen . . . told me who you guys are," Rusty said.

"With the eye overhead, help should be arriving." Noah eased his way to Sally. "How are you?"

"I've got a headache and my face isn't something you'll want to look at."

"I'll always want to look at your face," Noah said softly. "What happened?"

"You're sweet, Noah. I had a run in with Bucky and Rory. I want Rory."

"We can't count on help coming right now." Rusty patted his pockets. "Let's go through with my plan."

"What plan?"

Rusty told Noah of his plan and the agent agreed, "It's as good a plan as any — considering lack of time. Plus, the element of surprise is in our favor."

While the three prepared themselves, the eye of the storm passed, and the wind and rain picked up with a ferocity even the old-timers on Santa Rosa Island had never seen before. Kate commenced to finish what her first half started.

Noah gently pushed Cal and Rusty against the wall and eased closer to the mine chamber entrance. "I'll grab Bucky because he has the gun. Cal, Rusty, grab Wendy and your mothers. Sally, can you handle Rory?"

"With pleasure."

The three were at the opening when they heard a cry of pain from Bucky — then a slap of flesh against flesh and Wendy whimpering. "Hurry, Noah. This lil' wench bit me."

"Be quick." Noah pushed Rusty forward.

Rusty handed a cherry bomb to Cal and got a bottle rocket for himself. He lit both and the boys lobbed them into the chamber, followed by another cherry bomb and a spiral. Before the group inside knew what was happening, the whole chamber lit up in a blinding display of multi-colored lights.

"What the . . .?" Was all Rory could say.

"Let's go." Noah tapped the boys on their shoulders, then all four entered the chamber.

While there was still light from the fireworks Noah went straight for his brother while the boys went for their mothers. Wendy and Sally went for Rory.

"Noah?" McCoy rubbed his eyes. "What are you doin'?"

"Arresting you, Bucky, for human trafficking, kidnapping, child endangerment and murder. Need I go on?"

"You cain't. I'm yer brother."

"That doesn't mean a thing, Bucky. Ever since you got arrested for smuggling weed and got off, I've watched you. You don't take clients out all night for a fishing trip and you don't take them to a secret cove. And isn't it a coincidence that you told me the bank was ready to foreclose on your boat, yet you can afford to buy state-of-the-art radar and GPS? And isn't it a coincidence that there's an increase in the number of hungry, homeless people who can't speak English here in Pensacola?"

"Murder?" Cal's mother cried. "Bucky?"

"It seems Warren Chapman discovered Bucky's activities in human trafficking. And being a con-man and blackmailer he tried to blackmail these two." Noah nodded towards McCoy and Rory. "But of course Bucky and Rory wouldn't have it, so Bucky put Rory up to killing Warren. Wendy made the mistake of going below on the *SilverKing* and discovered something that put her in danger. What was it, Wendy?"

Wendy turned away, and barely able to speak, said, "It was *Captain Underpants' Attack of the Talking Toilets* — in Spanish."

"*Captain Underpants!* In Spanish no less!" Noah nodded to the rope Rory was going to use. "Bucky, you and Rory can barely read *The Little Engine That Could* in English — let alone Spanish."

"I was gonna lose the *SilverKing*. I only smuggled 'til I could get the gold."

The light from the fireworks was now gone, and before the two agents had a chance to turn their flashlights on, Bucky tried to escape. Unintentionally, Diane had her foot out and the old fishing guide tripped over it.

In the chaos Rory reached for the handgun, shoved Sally away, and crawled to the entrance of the chamber only to collide into Sheriff Raymond, two deputies and Mr. Sapp.

"Goin' somewhere?" The sheriff asked, shining his mag light over the chamber.

Rusty heard Mr. Sapp say, "Well Paul, looks like we've missed all the fun."

"Dad!" Cal and his mother ran to him while Rusty stepped over to Diane.

"Rusty, I'm so, so glad you're safe." She gave him a tight little hug. Did she mean it? He wondered. Time will tell.

Two more mag flashlights shined on the group and Rusty recognized the two men from the *SilverKing*. Rusty turned his attention to Wendy and noticed she was rubbing a bruise on her cheek while Cal held her. "He hit me, Cal."

"It's all over with, Wendy." Cal squeezed her. "And you've got Rusty to thank for saving us."

"Huh?" Wendy looked puzzled. How could a dweeb pull off such a stunt.

"Wendy," Diane said. "It was Rusty who made it in here and lit the firecrackers."

Mr. Sapp cradled his wife to his chest and ran his fingers through her long hair. "Becky, I was so worried about you. You didn't take your Nitro."

"I'm fine, Donnie," Ms. Sapp chuckled. "A little excitement was just what I needed."

Mr. Sapp turned to Rusty. "That was a brave but dumb thing you did." Mr. Sapp looked Rusty up and down. "You could've been killed."

"The others could've been killed too, sir."

"Yes, well, since everyone seems to be okay, ah'm turnin' this over to Sheriff Raymond."

The lawman looked at Sally, popped his gum and said, "Hmmm. I thought my wife looked rough in the morning."

Sally smiled in embarrassment and waved him off.

"Anyhow," Sheriff Raymond continued, "introductions appear to be in order. This lady, and she certainly is a lady, is Sally Jo Jensen, U.S. Treasury agent." The sheriff looked at Rory. "If any village had an idiot this guy would be it. Y'all know who he is. Now, these two guys . . ." The sheriff pointed to the two men who held Bucky and Rory. "Abbot and Costello, here, are agents Floyd Jackson and Danny Bauer. Chubby here . . ." The lawman walked over to Noah McCoy. "This is homegrown agent Noah McCoy. All are agents of the United States Treasury." Sheriff Reynolds looked at Sally. "Have their rights been read?"

"They have."

"Good. Git 'em out of here." Sheriff Raymond looked at Sally. "And let's git you to a doctor before all heck breaks loose.

Wendy looked at Noah McCoy. "Mr. McCoy, didn't Warren know you're Captain McCoy's brother?"

"Wendy, it didn't matter. To him I was just another ex-con looking for a easy way out.

"So, ye wanted to work with me just so you could catch me?" Bucky McCoy gave his brother an evil look.

"Like I said Bucky, we were watching you like a hawk."

Bucky looked down at the floor. "You know, Noah, Granpappy gave me the secret to the gold, because he knew you were a goody two-shoes. All my life I waited for the right moment to get it. Waited for someone greedy and stupid enough to dig for it. This Chapman guy and this kid comes along and I almost had it."

"Bucky, Granpappy was a lot like you. He told tall tales and taller tales when he was drunk. He said he was with Teddy Roosevelt when he charged San Juan Hill. Ha! Granpappy never left the United States and was charged with desertion. Think about that in prison." Noah walked over to Sally looked at her battered face then took her hand. "Are you okay?"

"Fine." Sally smiled. "How about you?"

"Okay. Just worried about you."

Rusty saw the look the two gave each other, and gave Cal a knowing look. Cal smiled and nodded back.

"I wonder how the RV did," Diane said.

Rusty took his mother's arm. "Let's get out of here and see."

"Wait, Rusty." Wendy walked over to him. "I had a gun pointed at me and was inches away from dying. It makes you think. As bad as I've treated you, you saved my life. Thank you, cousin." Wendy kissed him on the cheek.

Rusty stared at her a second. "Just don't call me anymore names and stop teasing me."

"I won't . . . What I mean is, I'll treat you right."

We'll never be close but at least the teasing and name-calling will stop, Rusty thought. And I'll try to see her . . . the way Cal sees her.

Only the echo of footsteps could be heard down the hall as an eerie quiet prevailed and Rusty could literally see the light at the end of the tunnel.

"Ms. Jensen —" Wendy kept in step with the Treasury agent. "Like . . . a . . . how did you get hooked up with Warren in the first place and since you were suppose to be husband and wife how did you keep him from . . ."

Wendy's face turned red. "You know."

Everyone laughed.

"Warren was an ex-con and had a record longer than your arm. His latest effort in his get rich quick schemes was trying to find hidden treasures. If not finding them legally — then stealing them. He almost got caught in Nevada in an abandoned mine. He came to Florida with it's miles of coast and folk tales of pirate gold. He heard the story of 'Geronimo's gold,' figured he could be successful and got you involved. It was time to move in. I met Warren at his favorite bar. We were never married, never slept together. It was all about the gold."

"But how did Rory and Captain McCoy do *that* to you?" Wendy asked, referring to the young agent's face.

"Warren wanted a scrapbook of all his activities. Rory came to the campsite and told me Bucky wanted to see me. They asked me about the gold and when I told them I didn't know anything they beat me. Bucky already had Wendy so I feigned unconsciousness when they left the boat. The storm was closing in so I had to move fast. Rusty, you were searching the fort and we kept missing each other. Rory went to dispose of some evidence and that's when he kidnapped Cal and everybody."

"You dog!" Noah lunged at Rory only to be restrained by Sheriff Raymond and the two other agents. "You never were a man, Rory. Get him out of my sight."

Rusty looked around. "Where's Norma Jean?"

"I set her free." Bucky choked. "What we were planning had no place for Norma Jean." He lowered his head. "I miss her already."

"That's about the only good thing you did recently," Cal snapped.

"Cal," Becky shook her head.

"Will you look at this?" Mr. Sapp waved his hand at the devastation. In the distance mobile homes were tossed any which way on their sides, upside down — sort of like toys. Roofs were totally or partially ripped off homes and businesses.

"It looks like a nuclear bomb hit," Cal whispered and clasped his mother's hand.

The road from Ft. Pickens to the campsite was impassable by car. Fallen trees, parts of homes, boats of all sizes and downed power lines made the way extremely hazardous. Rusty, his mother, Wendy and the Sapps inched their way on foot to the campground only to find an enormous limb laying on top of the crushed roof of the RV.

"It's totaled." Diane squeezed Rusty's hand. "I wonder if we have cell phone service. I've got to call your father."

While Diane called her husband, Noah wondered about the *SilverKing*. Cal and Rusty told him where the boat was and volunteered a quick trip to see how it fared.

The group found the boat aground with only a bent propeller.

Noah walked around the vessel and chuckled. "If that's all the damage is to it I can have it up and running in about a month." He looked at Sally. "That is, if I have the right help."

Rusty watched the coy expression on Sally's face. "What are you talking about?"

Noah smiled. "I think you know."

"So you really went to LSU?" Cal asked Sally as he ran his hand along the side of the boat.

"Yes. I majored in Criminal Justice and minored in business. Just right for an agent. I go to every Tiger game I can. And the best part?" Sally grew serious. "No more moldy bread."

Everyone looked at her but didn't say anything.

Diane told everyone that her husband was coming immediately. The Sapps offered Diane, Wendy and Rusty a place to stay until other arrangements could be made. To occupy their time, Rusty helped Cal and his father salvage what they could from the RV and helped clear debris from around the Sapp's home and Ft. Pickens.

"Look at that," Rusty said to Cal, pointing to Wendy who was picking up a plastic chair. "She's actually working for once."

"Don't knock it — and be grateful," Cal replied.

After destroying the Panhandle, Kate weakened as she moved inland then turned east dumping four to five inches of rain on Georgia before moving out to sea off Savannah. She gained a little of her strength back as she moved north before dying in the cold waters off Nova Scotia.

Once the hurricane left, only the National Guard, Red Cross, Salvation Army and property owners were allowed back on the island. The National Guard to protect against looters and render any possible aid, the Red Cross and Salvation Army to provide food, ice and shelter, the property owners to survey the damage and talk to insurance adjusters when they arrived.

Rusty's day, Jerry Parker, arrived the next day. He noticed the bruise on Wendy's cheek. "I forgot to ask, Rusty, Wendy . . . . How did you two get along?" Everyone chuckled. Jerry stood with his hands on his hips and looked from his wife to Rusty and Wendy.

The two cousins looked at each other. Wendy spoke up, "You could say we had some real fireworks." Wendy and Rusty burst out laughing.

MEDICINE MAN

Pensacola, Florida — January — Eighteen Months Later

A year and a half after settling in New Orleans, Wendy and the Parkers received subpoenas to appear as witnesses in the murder trial of Rory Abrams. Susan Terrell — now Susan Dubrois, and her new husband, were going on a cruise and could not be bothered to fly up to Pensacola with Wendy.

"What's wrong, honey?" Diane asked as she and Rusty waited for Wendy's plane.

"It's just . . . don't get me wrong, Mom." Rusty made a face. "I love Aunt Susan, but this is really an important day in Wendy's life. Don't you think she ought to be here?"

"I agree with you, Rusty. With all that happened you would think she would appreciate Wendy more. I tried talking to her but right now, and I hate to admit it, Wendy is excess baggage for her."

Rusty shook his head. "It's sad."

Wendy's plane arrived, and when the passengers disembarked Rusty could not believe his eyes. "What happened to your gothic clothes and all your rings?"

"I'm going with a really cool guy who doesn't like that stuff," Wendy said.

Rusty stared at Wendy's shiny, shoulder-length hair. "And your purple hair?"

"He doesn't like that either." Wendy sighed. "Randy is a redne . . . ah. . . country boy . . . whose parents own a big ranch in Hardee County. They're cool . . . and are like . . ." Wendy looked at Diane, "the mom and dad I never had."

"I'm so happy for you." Diane hugged her niece.

Wendy stepped back and sized Rusty up. "And what about you, Rusty? Looks like you've lost some weight."

"Yeah." Rusty sucked his stomach in. "I read where all that fat could kill you. After what we went through that summer, I'm not takin' any chances."

"Smart. Let's get my bags."

"Wendy," Rusty touched her arm. "I was wonderin'. Why did you hate me so much and call me all those names for so many years."

Wendy took a deep breath. "It's all in the past, Rusty. But now, since I'm going with a great guy and have things in my life together, I'll admit I was a jealous of you. How I envied you. You have everything Rusty. I mean . . . parents who love you, who guide you. The only male in my life despised me. Even Byron, my new stepfather isn't around for me. When I have a question he just says 'later', but later never comes. Cal was right, I was looking for male acceptance. It's by the grace of God that Randy sees I'm somebody special and I'm worth something. I have all the stuff money can buy, but my parents have nothing to do with me. Randy's parents are the ones who love me, show me the way, tell me what's right and wrong."

Wendy looked directly into Rusty's eyes. "All I can say is I'm sorry. And thank you for forgiving me."

Rusty picked up one of Wendy's bags. "As you said, it's all in the past."

The trial began the next day with only a few spectators.

While waiting for the judge to appear Rusty noticed Noah and Sally walk into the courtroom. Sally, Diane, Wendy and Becky Sapp embraced each other.

"Lookit that rock!" Cal's father exclaimed.

Sally held out her hand. "Noah and I were married just two months ago."

"Congratulations!" The women nearly shouted.

"Thank you. We retired from the Treasury."

"Really?" Diane asked.

"Yes. When Noah came back to Santa Rosa Island, the lure of the sea got too much for him. He took over the *SilverKing* and is a fishing guide."

"Wonderful."

"All rise." The balliff's voice filled the courtroom.

Wendy, under oath, admitted she was mesmerized by Rory's good looks and smooth talk. She said she was amazed that such a handsome guy would want to marry her. The prosecution presented Rory as a shiftless, lazy opportunist looking for an easy way out and willing to do anything for it — even murder. The defense painted Rory as a victim of society with a stern unforgiving father and a meek mother, and that Rory was a misguided young man with no notion of right or wrong who fell under the influence of his brother Bucky McCoy. The jury didn't buy it.

It only took a day and a half for the trial to be over and a verdict reached. Rory Abrams was found guilty of murder, kidnapping, human trafficking and child endangerment. He was sentenced to life in prison without parole.

Bucky McCoy's trial would begin in another month and by all indications, it did not look good for him.

Santa Rosa Island — Later That Week

The Parkers were standing outside the Sapp's home, where the loblolly bay tree once stood, when and old, rusty, blue and white Ford pick-up squeaked to a stop. A tall lanky man climbed out wearing a Stetson hat, a heavy ranch jacket, cowboy boots and jeans. His black hair was tied back in a ponytail. A pair of round sunglasses, popular back in the sixties, hung low on his nose.

Mr. Sapp walked over and wrapped his arm around the man's shoulder. "This here is Dr. Vincent Dunn of Florida State. Besides bein' an ol' buddy of mine, Vinny teaches Native American History at the university. He's an expert on Geronimo and the Apaches. Vinny is gonna lay this Geronimo gold thing to rest once and for all."

After shaking hands with everyone Dr. Dunn said, "We might as well get started."

As the group drove to Ft. Pickens, Dr. Dunn spoke of Geronimo's life on the plains and his life after he became a prisoner. "Geronimo's Chiricahua name was 'Foyahkla' ('One Who Yawns') After his family was killed by Mexicans in March of 1851, Geronimo had a vision. He heard a voice say that no guns would ever kill him. And believe it or not . . ." Dr. Dunn smiled. "The guns of his enemies nearly always jammed or misfired."

"Remarkable." Rusty's father remarked, shaking his head.

Dr. Dunn turned a corner. "You see . . . after his family was killed, he had an almost a pathological hatred for the Mexicans."

"I guess you can understand how he felt . . . ," Rusty said.

Tapping the wheel for emphasis, Dr. Dunn continued, "And Geronimo could see things. Almost in the future — with uncanny accuracy."

The professor told of how Geronimo petitioned for better conditions in the prison at Ft. Pickens and Ft. Sill. And he told how Geronimo rode in the 1902 Inaugural parade of President Teddy Roosevelt. He asked the President to send the Apaches back to Arizona. And then the now-famous Apache joined *Buffalo Bill's Wild West Show* and became a tourist attraction.

At Ft. Pickens, Rusty and Cal carried a large box Dr. Dunn had brought with him to the spot where they were going to dig. They watched the professor survey the area where the south wall, destroyed by the hurricane, used to be.

"Now," Dr. Dunn addressed Mr. Sapp. "You told me the quarters in the south wall were demolished after Geronimo went to Arizona, correct?"

"Correct."

"Alright." The professor walked to the box, opened it and handed each member of the group a spade. He then produced four artist brushes and two sifters made of 2x4s and metal screen.

The professor laid the sifters on the ground. "I don't think we'll need these, but just in case, here's what I want you to do. Wendy, Rusty, Cal, Don. Dig very carefully around the area — a little at a time. If we don't find anything we'll move a little further out. If anything was there, unless someone picked it up, it should still be there."

The group decided who should dig where and began digging. For the second time in his life, Rusty watched Wendy do manual labor and not complain.

Two hours later, with no one finding anything and a cold front beginning to come though, the group wrapped up for the day.

They had dinner at a newly reopened Olive Garden on the mainland.

"It's good to see the progress Santa Rosa County is making." Jerry Parker bit into a breadstick.

"It's takin' time but we're makin' it." Cal's father took a sip of iced tea.

Wendy twirled her pasta around her fork and burst out laughing.

"What's so funny?" Cal asked.

"I was just thinking about the pelican. Remember when she counted for us?"

Rusty jabbed a tomato. "Yeah. She was a pretty smart bird."

Diane dipped her spoon in a cup of gnocchi soup, stirred it and studied it intently.

"What's wrong, baby?" Rusty's dad asked.

"Something Sally said at the boat." Diane didn't take her eye off the breadstick. "Something about no more moldy bread."

"Mom, Sally told me she was so poor as a child that her family had to go through grocery store dumpsters to get something to eat. If they found a loaf of moldy multi-grain bread her family considered it a real treat."

Rusty took a sip of iced tea.

Mr. Sapp pushed his plate away. "Ah'm glad she made something of herself so she won't be hungry anymore."

Becky Sapp took a sip of hot tea. "So am I."

"And we have so much," Diane murmured. "We don't even know how many people are going hungry right in our own neighborhood."

Everyone was silent for moment, lost in thought.

Dr. Dunn reached for the bill. "If everyone's finished I suggest we get a good night's sleep. We've got a lot of work to do tomorrow."

At the motel everyone said goodnight.

The next thing Rusty knew it was morning.

By eleven a.m., the group had the whole front of where the south Ft. Pickens wall used to be dug up and hadn't found a thing. Rusty poured his spade full of sand and concrete onto a small pile, stood, stretched and pulled his jacket tighter. With the temperature in the upper thirties, it felt good to move and keep warm.

"I'm gonna start at the corner," Rusty yelled to Dr. Dunn and knelt on the other side of the fort.

"Here you are, Rusty's dad said, offering cups of hot tea to everyone.

"Thanks." Rusty took a sip and started digging.

He dug one more spade full then heard Wendy cry, "I found something!"

Everyone dropped what they were doing and ran to her. She knelt, holding a small, cracked leather pouch. "Do you think this is the over one-hundred-year-old pouch that caused so much trouble?"

Dr. Dunn reached for the pouch. "I think this is it, Wendy."

A captivating feeling crept over Rusty. Here was a pouch placed there by a legend. A legend whose face and life were part of history. Rusty bit his lip and squeezed his hands. In a few seconds maybe they would know if there ever was Geronimo's gold.

Dr. Dunn looked at each person. "Shall we?"

Everyone nodded.

"Come here, Wendy and hold your hands out." He untied the pouch and gently poured it's contents, one item at a time, into Wendy's hands. First came a downy, eagle feather followed by an abalone shell. Last was a small bag of what looked like pollen.

There was a moment of absolute silence.

"That's it?" Rusty asked.

"That's it," Dr. Dunn replied.

"No gold?" Wendy tried to hide her disappointment.

Dr. Dunn stood up. "No gold. Just as I thought."

"Why not?" Wendy asked.

"You must remember, Wendy, Geronimo was not a chief. He didn't need gold to do his job. He had these three objects because he had what the Apaches referred to as the *Power*. And Geronimo only became a warrior after his family was killed. First and foremost, Geronimo was a medicine man."

"What was the shell and feather used for?" Wendy asked.

"The Chiricahuas had a ceremony for almost everything in life To please and appeal to the spirits," Dr. Dunn replied.

"But the . . . Pollen . . .?" Wendy asked.

"Geronimo had an old black basket filled with the tools he needed for each ritual. The pollen was used in healing. Geronimo would roll . . ."

"Like a cigarette?" Rusty interrupted.

Dr. Dunn nodded. "Yes, I guess so. And he puffed it in the direction of the four winds. He would then rub the pollen onto the patient and pray to the four winds."

"Would the patient survive?" Wendy asked.

"Well . . ." Professor Dunn looked up at the sky. "There was at least one case when Geronimo spread the pollen on the upper body of a patient and told him he'd get well — and he did."

"Wow! Rusty said.

"Why do you think he hid the pouch here."

"Geronimo probably thought the Army would take it from him. After all, they took everything else. He no doubt assumed that one day he would return to Ft. Pickens and retrieve it. Or maybe . . . he had plenty of time to cut away the mortar, he simply pulled out a brick, put the pouch in the wall then replaced the brick."

"That's what Bucky McCoy's great-grandfather saw," Wendy yelled.

"Quite possibly." Dr. Dunn replaced the contents to the pouch, tied it and handed it to Wendy. "Put it way, way down in the earth."

After Wendy buried the pouch, Jerry Parker put his hands on Wendy and Rusty's shoulders. "We better head back. New Orleans is a long way from here." He shook the men's hands. "Thanks for everything."

Halfway across the three-mile bridge the cousins spotted a man and woman in a boat with three other people. The cousins could barely make out the name *SilverKing* on the stern. Wendy and Rusty waved to the couple. Noah and Sally waved back as they headed into the Gulf.

Suggested Reading

Geronimo by Angie Debo.

Hurricanes by Patrick J. Fitzpatrick was extremely helpful.

ACKNOWLEDGMENTS

Geronimo and his Apaches were indeed prisoners at Ft. Pickens but the pouch and gold are products of my imagination.

I would like to thank the weather people at ABC7 for taking time from their busy schedule to talk to me about hurricanes. A heartfelt thanks to the people of Pensacola for their warm hospitality. Thanks to the staff of Corkscrew Swamp Sanctuary, we both had a good laugh when I asked how much water a pelican's pouch can hold. Thanks to ladies at the Ft. Myers Library for their help in finding me information on Hurricane Hunters. Any errors are mine — not theirs.

Thanks to my editor and publisher Doris Wenzel who suggested I travel to Santa Rosa Island. Thanks to my critique group — Mary Beth, Joan and Karyn for their input. Thanks to Nancy Mane and Larry Lucas for their opinions. Last, but not least, thanks to my family Sandy, Matthew and Tara for being there and believing. I couldn't have done it without y'all.

Mark C. Pilles
May, 2013

Other Books for Older Children and Young Adults published by Mayhaven Publishing, Inc.

A Doorway Through Space (Judith Bourassa Joy)

Beyond the Road (Margee Bugbee Howe)

Crossover Dribble (P.J. Farris)

Crusin' Sarah (Yoli)

Elizabeth Terwilliger: Someone Special (Phyllis Stanley)

Following the Raven (Jenny Weaver)

Jigsaw - Second in the Olde Locke Mysteries (Terri A. DeMitchell)

Kid Posse & The Phantom Robber (R. Kent Tipton)

Mystery of the Missing Candlesticks (June Weltman)

Phillip and the Boy Who Said "Huh?" (John Paulits)

Presidents from the Prairie State (Pamela J. Farris)*

Pythagorus Eagle & the Music of the Spheres (Anne Carse Nolting)

More Books for Older Children and Young Adults published by Mayhaven Publishing, Inc.

The Petticoat Soldier (Nancy Polette)

The Portsmouth Alarm (Terri A. DeMitchell)

The Rawleigh Man Told Me (Ruth St. John Thomas)

The Wishflower Field (Jennifer Fallaws)

Valley of the Flames (Herman H. White)

Who Shot the Spatzies (Margaret Clem)

World's Greatest Star Trek Quiz (Nan Clark)

You Will Come Back - First in the Olde Locke Mysteries (Terri A. DeMitchell)